NEVER WITHOUT YOU

The Letter Club – Book 3

Elle Wright

PRAISE FOR THE LETTER CLUB

Nothing Else But You

"This was one of my favorites from an author period. It had everything I love in a novel. The characters and plot had me from beginning to end. Highly recommend." ~JuliaBookLandReviews

"I totally fell in love with this book, Gio is a dream and so is his girl. We get to know them through their letters and want them to get on in real life despite all the possible problems and obstacles. My new favourite author." ~JennyIndigo

"Wow! Loved it. I found the letters so great for a written style. The couple finding out about each other and falling in love without ever meeting. Awesome characters with so much emotion. A must read!" ~Laura Johnston

"This story was so touching. The plot is emotionally brilliant and the characters fit in perfectly. I love the emotional vulnerability and chemistry the protagonists have." ~PinkieIsShy

"Old fashioned letter writing has never been done better." ~Loni

If Ever I Fall

"The second book in "The Letter Club" series does not disappoint. I have to admit that I am a sucker for an old fashioned letter, so this story was right up my alley. If the idea of breaking out pen and paper seems archaic to you, then you may want to skip it.....but why on Earth would you want to do that? You would miss a phenomenal love story. Matteo is the love interest that everyone is looking for and Sophia is the girl that makes his heart melt." ~RomanceReaderHB82

"If Ever I Fall is a great romantic read of a woman escaping harm's way, far away from her new love. The only way to stay in touch is through love letters. She learns more and loves more through the love letters. Love From Afar Makes The Heart Grow Stronger. Great Read." ~Amanda Enriquez

"If Ever I Fall is about the romance between Sofia and Matteo by Elle Wright filled with danger, romance, and suspense. I became intrigued after reading the description to find out who Matteo was and what the truth about Sofia's family was. I was really surprised at the answers but you would have to read the book to find out." ~Nadia

"I enjoyed this new "Letter Club" story! It's an amazing read that is wonderfully developed and nicely written. I love the characters in this slow burn read. Matt and Sophia are so good together. What a match made for each other and a great love story with suspense, romance, danger and so much more." ~Mary

www.BOROUGHSPUBLISHINGGROUP.com

NEVER WITHOUT YOU
Copyright © 2020 Elle Wright

ISBN 978-1-951055-81-3

Reach for the sweet, it tastes like love…

ACKNOWLEDGMENTS

To the mental health professionals who have the compassion, empathy, and skill that help people overcome all types of traumas. Your work is quiet, but oh so critical.

To the good and honest first responders who keep us safe from all manner of danger. We haven't forgotten you, and we are sad the worst among you overshadow the men and women who put their lives on the line for their communities and country.

Thanks to my beta reader, aka Miss Honesty. 'Preciate you more than you know.

To Boroughs Publishing Group, thank you for being there.

NEVER WITHOUT YOU

Dutchford, Connecticut
Theresa
Fluent in Neanderthal

I knew what I was doing before I did it, yet I went ahead with it, knowing I shouldn't do it.

That right there was evidence enough I'd lost my mind. Convoluted thinking was not my stock-in-trade. Clearheaded, sensible, responsible, well-respected in my profession, empathetic, and compassionate were some of the many words, accolades, kindnesses tossed my way on a regular basis. Alas, that shit flew out the window a few months ago.

Allow me to backtrack. Actually, you should start at the beginning, as I did seven months ago.

A patient of mine – there's a shifting characterization here, but I'll get to that later – told me about The Letter Club and I was intrigued. After everything I'd been through, the ability to connect with people, or, if I was being honest, maybe form a connection with a special someone anonymously, would be a godsend. No one would know who I was, where I was, and what had happened fifteen months ago that changed my life irrevocably. The idea that I would be assigned a correspondence number and all the letters went through The Letter Club appealed on every level. TLC forwarded the mail to their various members, keeping their identities confidential. Exactly what I was looking for.

I signed up, got my number, and penned my first letter – eleven drafts until I finally gave up and mailed what I had – which they sent out to hundreds of people who'd answered questionnaires as I had, defining their interests and preferences, which, allegedly, matched up with mine. After sending out the first missive, all I had to do was sit back and wait for return mail.

My First Letter

Dear You,

Genuinely pleased to meet you. I came inside a little while ago after planting new seasonal flowers in pots and bowls scattered on my back patio. It takes me forever at the garden center to decide what to buy because I want one, or ten, of everything. But I'm dealing with limited space, and not being a great visualizer creates choice conundrums. I knew I'd been standing in an aisle staring at the overhead netting for too long when the third person in a green apron and a floppy hat asked me if I needed help. Forced to commit, I wound up buying four colors of a long-lasting variety of a flowering plant. I was so pleased with myself for making the selection I loaded up my cart but forgot to buy orchid soil. I'm a sucker for orchids, and have a bunch already, so when a neighbor asked if I wanted a few more, which she admitted to swiping off the tables at the end of some work-related party, I couldn't say no. Now I have six little orchid plants in dire need of re-potting sitting on a kitchen counter. A perfect excuse to return to the garden center where I'll stand in an aisle staring into space again, but I swear, I'll get the orchid soil first.

What's going on in your world?
#1,278,642

My fifteenth response: the other fourteen were written by…nuts, and that's my professional opinion.

Yeah, I'm not calling you #1,278,642. You're Flower. Writing isn't my thing, but I have the kind of job that makes it hard to meet people, and a couple I know met this way and they're happy, so I thought, why not?

Pick a name and I'll answer to it.

See, here's where being a therapist, as in shrink, gives me an edge. People often say a lot about themselves even when they say hardly anything. Even without the ability to read his body language, without a doubt I know the man who wrote those fifty words – and yes, I'm certain a man wrote that note – is used to telling people what to do, but is more yielding than he'll admit, and he wants to meet someone and be happy. I'm used to helping people discover things about themselves, which helps them explain their behavior. I have to be flexible because everyone sorts through the detritus of their lives differently, and I listen with an open mind with the understanding my job is to lead them where they need to go to get better.

Although I wasn't "shrinking" a potential friend, I felt in this man's case, I'd follow his lead. Sometimes giving away control actually allows a person to have more power because they decide what they're giving and why. I know, I know, occupational hazard analyzing every move, but I don't do it with the people I love and trust. Those relationships are organic, even if some of them are fraught with familial drama. This guy needs to feel like he is on top of a situation over which he has no control. I'll start my next letter with a name I think he'll answer to while amusing myself. Ross rhymes with boss, and this guy definitely wants to be in charge.

Dear Ross,

Thank you for your note and the name. It's appropriate, and sort of sixties-ish at the same time. One of my former college roommates name is Windsong. Pretty, but it screams Jefferson Airplane and communes. Her parents are free spirits with a hippie throwback vibe. Wendy, which she prefers, is the antithesis of everything her upbringing encouraged. She's careful, deliberate, shy, and has a PhD in biomedical engineering. No living off the land on an organic farm for her. She's button-down, organized, and methodical. I've had dinner with her and her family a couple of times. It's painful for her, even though her two brothers, who take after their parents, and her parents try to make her feel loved and comfortable.

I'm in no danger of being turned away by my parents or my sister if I told them my new name is Flower. They'll shorten it to Flo in a heartbeat then carry on as if it was the name I was born with.

In case you are wondering, I went back to the garden center and got the orchid soil, and put the little orchids in a large bowl-shaped planter. I'm hoping they like their new home and produce lots of blooms. And, yes, I did some staring into space, but my wandering mind latched onto the need for a couple of new blue hydrangeas, another favorite of mine.

Looking forward to hearing what's going on in your world.
Flower

Twenty-five days later:

Flower,
Nothing to say. I don't know why I bothered.
Ross

Well, I didn't expect that, but it told me a lot about him. He had nothing to say, almost didn't answer – the two-week delay in receiving the note – but he wants me to know what he's thinking so he bothered to write to tell me he had nothing to say. This guy wants to dance, but he's afraid (I love this phrase so I'm using it) to bust a move. Something's got him all hemmed up inside, but he wants to push past it. I'm intrigued. I get to be a psychological detective without any repercussions. This is more fun than I expected it would be.

Ross,
Why did you bother?
Flower

Twelve days later:
The netting.

See, he wants to talk, but loquacious is not a word attributable to him. Yeah, I know, I'm the mistress of understatement. He wrote back quickly, which tells me he's into continuing the conversation. I figure I'll answer in kind.

What about the netting?

Thirteen days later:
You knew you were going to the garden center. You knew you needed new flowers. You had to know the capacity of your patio and what looked good there, but you went out unprepared and had no problem standing in the middle of a store there, but not there. The ability to let go and lose yourself in thought in a public place got me. That's why I bothered.

Oh yeah. This is all about control. This guy's every daily move is plotted and examined. Me letting go and zoning out in a garden center knocked against his carefully constructed life in a way that appealed to him. Writing letters through TLC is a huger thing for him than I thought. Taking a chance writing to me, clearly someone who doesn't have his level of control issues, is a risk he's willing to take. I'm going to start rattling his well-constructed sense of stability. Nothing big, but I want to see how far he's willing to go outside his comfort zone. He has no idea what a big deal this is for me, but I'm well practiced at keeping my feelings from showing. Can you imagine what my patients would think if they could read my thoughts and feelings on my face? I wouldn't have any patients.

Ross,

Well, a garden center isn't just any public place. While I know nowhere is completely safe, the likelihood something is going to happen to me in this garden center is pretty low, especially a garden center that's only a garden center. Where I go isn't attached to a big box store. It's a family business that's been in the area for around fifty years. I think the grandkids are running the place now, and it still has the feel of a hometown store. I bump into a lot of familiar faces when I'm there, so I feel safe, and being relaxed seems second nature. Mind you, I fall asleep on public transportation all the time. If it's moving and I'm not the driver, I get lulled to sleep. I know it's not ideal, as in people around me are generally strangers, but in an airplane there's limited exposure so it's not too bad, but trains can be dicey. I try to stay awake, but it's a struggle.

In other news, a midsummer disaster: the AC in my office building crashed, and for three days going to work was unbearable. We had fans blowing everywhere, but all that did was move the hot air around from one place to another. It's one of those sealed buildings where you can't open the windows. No sucking out the stale hot air. It's fixed now, and the reaction to having been without the AC is now they've cranked it up. We're freezing, and I have to wear a sweater or a jacket in the office to keep my lips from turning blue. Talk about going from one extreme to the other. Enough people have complained, and I'm interested to learn what climate I'm going to be working in tomorrow. I might have to leave a couple of changes of clothes to keep up with in-office temperature fluctuations.

Flower

Ten days later:
Woman, stop riding trains if you fall asleep. Don't be so damn casual about your safety. Do you know how many crimes are committed on subways and commuter rail lines, never mind long-distance hauls? From the way it sounds, you're riding the trains alone and falling asleep. You're a sitting duck. A prime target. Quit doing that shit right now or you won't be around to plant blue hydrangeas.
Ross

That got to me in a way I didn't expect. Although I can profile this man – that note suggests he works in or has worked in some type of law enforcement agency – I don't know him, and he sure doesn't know me. Yet, the forcefulness of his insistence felt intimate. As if he was genuinely worried about my safety. That he cares. If a five-line note can evoke those emotions, now I'm wondering what being with this guy would be like. I don't need someone to make me feel safe, but I'd love having that. Especially after what I've lived though. I know I'll never meet him, much less spend any time with him, but the thought that he would take care of me that way gave me comfort, and hope. Without saying too much, I felt compelled to respond to his note, and to reassure him.

Ross,
Actually, I'm not casual about my safety. I understand the randomness of life, and have a healthy respect for how everything can go from sugar to shit in the blink of an eye. I can't promise I won't ride trains ever again, but I will try to have a companion with me if I do. Lately, I've been driving almost everywhere, and I don't anticipate that changing anytime in the near future.
Thank you for caring.
Flower

Ten days later:
Tell me what happened.

Ross

I didn't think I'd said enough for him to extrapolate I'd lived through a trauma, but apparently I was wrong. Clearly, he's smart and intuitive, and definitely connected to law enforcement somehow if he saw more than I intended to communicate. Regardless of his empathy and probable knowledge about the effects of what I'd experienced, I have no intention of sharing. The minute I say anything, he'll know who I am. I'd made national news. It wouldn't take a computer genius to dig up the sordid details. The whole purpose of using TLC was to keep my identity hidden. I wasn't about to do or say anything to change that. I needed to turn the conversation and steer him away from the truth.

Ross,

I appreciate you asking, but there's nothing to tell. The nature of my job brings me in contact with people who face all kinds of struggles, plus, no one who reads the papers or watches the news can escape the violence inflicted on the innocent. I drive more now than use public transportation because of a change in work location – I'm closer to home, which is a good thing.

Speaking of driving, I've been negotiating with a few friends I've known since grade school about who's driving this year to the beach house one of the group lives in year-round. It's an annual Labor Day weekend ritual that started in high school when we went to the same house, which, at the time, belonged to our friend's grandmother. Unfortunately, when we were in college, her grandmother died, and our friend inherited the house.

Most years we rotate the driving duty, but a couple of us have moved away from the area and they need to fly to get here. Coordinating the airport pickup with everyone's schedule and the vehicle size has proved challenging. Between the emails, texts, Skypes, and FaceTiming it seems like we're a UN delegation with protocols to follow. Last night we were laughing so hard during a group Skype, we never came to a consensus. I'm committed to nailing this down tonight.

Flower

Twelve days later:

Bullshit. I'll wait 'til you're ready to tell me. As for your group gig, unless you want to dick around for another week, all of you chip in, rent a Suburban, do the airport p/u together, and head to the beach.
Ross

We'd come to a similar solution three days before his letter arrived. As for him calling bullshit, I'm having a hard time thinking of how to answer him or if I should answer him ever again. I've never met a man so incisive, and I haven't even really met this guy. If he can see through me after a few meager pieces of correspondence, I shudder to think of what being with him in person would be like. Raw. Unyielding. A relationship with him would require me to lay myself bare, and I sure as shit wasn't ready for that. But he'd given me an out. Maybe I'll take it. But first I was going to hang with my girls. Four days with them will give me perspective. I had no intention of telling them about him. Hell, there was nothing to tell, not really. Okay. I'm lying. Fuck it. I'm going to engage in avoidance behavior for a few blissful days. Then I'll see how I feel.

Seventeen days later:
Didn't take you for a chicken, babe.
R

Obviously, I didn't write back and he called me on it. The long weekend with my girls had been fantastic. They were my security blanket. When all the bad stuff went down, they didn't coddle me, and they made sure I knew they loved me, warts and all. Seeing them and having that warmth, love, and acceptance face-to-face made me love them even more.

After I got home, I decided I didn't need more stress in my life. I'd been through the kind of ordeal that would never go away no matter how healthy my mind and body became.

The letters were supposed to be fun. Easy. Light flirting. Entertaining. A happy distraction. Plenty more responses had come in after I'd sent out my first letter. Surely someone in that unopened pile would fit my requirements.

But damn. That taunt. And *babe*? While I might be fluent in Neanderthal, it didn't mean I tolerated it.

My darling sweetie pie,

Stop throwing your bearskins on the cave floor when you get home from work.

Boston, Massachusetts
Ethan
Babe by any other name

The move across the country screwed up the mail. Her response, which usually takes about ten days, didn't arrive for nearly four weeks. Worth the wait, though it would've been better to've heard from her right way. Her answer fuckin' cracked me up. I knew she was a kick in the ass from that first letter. She'd started out playing at flighty, and I get that. Initially, most people try not to come on too strong. But I've been trained to read between the lines, and what I saw in her first two letters was one determined woman. I knew if we met, I'd be into her, and in a remarkable change of character, I wussed for a week when I felt myself wanting to know her in a way that wasn't typical. Then I thought of dropping the whole Letter Club thing.

But I didn't want her to stop writing.

The way she "spoke" in her letters was like a voice in my head, and that voice was smoky and sultry. And she knew how to lure me back, which meant she had skills. I'm not an easy man to deal with, and my job is unforgiving. Anyone clever enough to get my attention is worth the trouble. So, when she'd backed off after I'd pressed her to tell me what she'd survived, I knew the best way to get her attention was to tweak her. "Babe" would surely piss her off more than calling her "chicken," and damn if it didn't work. The woman is funny, and she doesn't back down.

I've always loved women. Females intrigue me. As the younger of two boys, my mother – who doesn't know the definition of shy or retiring – amazed me with her energy, efficiency, her ability to care, and, most of all, the way she loved my dad. The feeling was mutual, and as I grew up and learned how fucked-up other kids' lives were, I felt lucky for what I had at home. I know what devotion looks like, and had decided at a young age never to settle for anything less.

As a kid, my brother was wild and got into a shit-ton of trouble. I learned from his mistakes how to work around rules without blowing shit up in everyone's face. The stealth approach to life included watching and observing people before wading into any situation. Which is how I came to be fascinated with females.

Regardless of shape, size, ethnicity, color, age, or personality type, females have an innate sense of how to get their way. Some are bulldozers, and some are wily, but unless they've been traumatized or had their spirit beaten out of them, they could work a guy over and ninety percent of the time, he never knew what hit him, but he loved what she was giving him.

By the time I was interested in getting acquainted with female body parts, I'd caught on to most of the signals and signs when a girl was weaving her magic. Sometimes I played along, sometimes I walked away, but most of the time I engaged, using their sensibilities to my best advantage.

Which was how, by the time I got to high school, I'd earned a reputation as a player. Girls talk. They share, warn, and advise their sisters, cousins, and friends. I grew up in a small community where little stayed secret, but nothing compared to the communication web high school girls constructed, nurtured, and maintained. Yet in spite of, or because of, the warnings and advice, there was never a time I didn't have a willing female companion, unless I didn't want one.

Little changed in college, except the pool of possibles was wider and deeper, and the repercussions didn't crop up as often. My sophomore year my brother entered the police academy, and shortly before he graduated, he was offered a job with the Portland PD.

I'd gone to the graduation, and a few weeks later – I was attending U of O, less than two hours to Portland – he gave me a tour of the PD. I was hooked.

I'd been a languages major in the REEES program – Russian, East European, and Eurasian Studies – in college. My family was originally from a small town east of St. Petersburg, and from a future employment standpoint, I'd thought being fluent in Russian and knowing the culture would give me a leg up. I wasn't wrong. My language skills and knowledge base got me into the FBI Joint Terrorism Task Force way earlier than a lot of cops vying for the posting who'd had more years under their belts.

Keeping myself entertained with women – Portland was a bigger pool to draw from than college and hey, the uniform didn't hurt – after becoming a cop wasn't a problem, but once I joined the task force, my life changed.

I'm no literature major, and Shakespeare isn't my thing, but the line "There are more things in heaven and Earth, Horatio, than are dreamt of in your philosophy" couldn't be more true. Every day, shit is happening in the world that the public doesn't know about, and should never know about. The landscape of extremists, threats, and terror-based organizations shifts faster than dunes in a sandstorm, and new players enter the field, which makes keeping the civilian population safe a challenge not unlike wrangling venomous snakes.

With my language and cultural skills, as well as family ties – albeit remote – in a hot region, I became enmeshed in the task force. Work became my life. Sex was easy enough to come by, and I found myself wanting more but didn't have the time to invest in a relationship. Four years after joining the task force, the city of Portland pulled out of the JTFF, and I went back to being a detective. When the FBI offered me a position in their Boston office, I jumped at the opportunity.

I'd been instrumental in helping bring down a Ukrainian crime ring near Boston, and after the bust, a good friend who works in the Boston office was promoted to Supervisory Special Agent. He wanted me in his unit, and I wanted to go. I didn't think my life would be less complicated or I'd have a hellava lot more time, but I could invest in writing letters to a woman who had somehow gotten under my skin.

Hey babe,

Don't get your panties in a knot. I get you think babe is pejorative, but aside from using it to tweak you into answering me, I mean it warmly.

Appreciated the laugh. Your note cracked me up. Delay in answering is all mail related. I moved across the country recently. I've heard men are less adaptable to change than women. IDK if that's true, but I can't imagine anyone enjoying moving. Pain in the ass and nothing but upheaval. Adjusting to the job change – reason for the move – has been almost seamless, but finding my shit has been a nightmare. I'm not home enough to devote more than an hour a night to unpacking and sorting, so I'm good with one set of dishes and utensils, and one pan for a while.

How're the plants doing?

Ross

Eleven Days Later

Ross,

Well color me surprised. I thought you'd taken umbrage and had thrown in the towel. Good to know you have a sense of humor.

I don't mind babe if it's meant to be warm, but you have to admit: many men use it as a diminutive, especially in the workplace.

The flowers are flourishing under constant care and attention. I feed and water them when I come home from work, then sit out on the back patio with my dog, Boo, and enjoy the beauty. FYI Boo's not named after Boo Radley from To Kill a Mockingbird, or after the band with the same name. He's not white, so it's not a ghost thing. He was timid when I rescued him from the local shelter, and his name was a play on his character. Over time, he's come out of his shell. I take him to doggie day care twice a week so he's not alone all the time when I'm at work, and the socializing helps. Now, he's quite territorial about the house and back patio, and his name fits because he tries to scare off people while he goes about his protection duties, which he takes seriously. The vet thinks he's about three years old and is some kind of a doodle blend. I could get a DNA test done to find out his breed lineage, but I don't care. He's sweet, and I love him no matter his parentage.

I agree about moving. As I've mentioned, my office relocated, and while it wasn't across the country, and it's one room with limited personal stuff compared to moving a household, I hated it nonetheless. But, once it was done, and I got set up and organized, I was happy for the change.

Wherever it is you are, try to get out and enjoy your new surroundings. All work and no play makes Ross a dull caveman.

Flower

Oh yeah. I could really get into this woman. Something about the way she phrases things, there's a real empathy there that's ingrained in her. I bet she's sweet down to her soul. Sucks major I can't be with her in person, but sucks more if I could. I wouldn't be able to give her the time she deserves, and this woman should have a man's undivided attention.

Work has been crazy busy. There are more bad people in the world than anyone could imagine, and they're crawling all over college campuses either recruiting or studying us. Total fluke, we got wind of a group of Russian students at Boston University through Skip's – my friend/supervisor – kid, Jonas. He'd come home to do laundry, and was ranting about some douches who are on his floor in the dorms and how they always have twenty of their friends over getting drunk, loud, really obnoxious with the girls, and doing it all in Russian.

In and of itself, the story didn't send up any red flags. Lots of kids were obnoxious in college, and students from a repressed society, more so. But one thing Jonas had told his dad made Skip sit up and pay attention. Apparently people were coming and going at all hours, and one night Jonas was studying late, left his room to use the bathroom, and saw an older guy, someone who was definitely not college age, slip a manila envelope under the exchange students' door. Then, a few days later, when Jonas was going out for his morning run, he witnessed the same guy hanging by the dorm way early.

Jonas said, "The dude is twitchy and doesn't look right."

According to Skip, Jonas is as far away from being law enforcement material as a person can be. He's laid-back, a tech nerd, doesn't pay much attention to his surroundings, and thinks the FBI is big brother. For Jonas to make the observations he had set off Skip's alarm bells. After running it by their Assistant Special Agent-in-Charge (ASAC), they got the green light to start looking into these bozos.

Since this shit is right up my alley, I got the case, and now I and my team of two other special agents are surveilling about twenty-five male Russian students at Boston University.

Sometimes, when I'm lying in bed trying to shut down my brain, I go back to my family home in Fiddler's Rest and think about the life my parents gave us. I want that for myself. Someone to come home to every night who I love and loves me: someone who's happy to see me when I drag my ass home. A house filled with kids and dogs. A life filled with love, comfort, and laughter.

Skip has that, but the trouble is not many agents or cops do. The divorce rate is high in law enforcement for a reason. Those of us who wear a badge are tied to our jobs in a way most people aren't.

It's not the kind of work you can leave at the office, and when you're called out in the middle of the night, not only can't you say no, most of the time you're rushing to get to wherever it is you're being sent.

I'm thirty-four years old, and since college I haven't been with anyone for more than a couple of months.

Hey babe,

I'm envious – you have Boo. Everyone needs a dog. I grew up with five of them over time. Two Golden Retrievers when I was little. Perfect dogs for small children: patient and tolerant. When they died, we got a Great Dane that was huge and tore up the yard so bad my folks didn't want two dogs. Elvis was enough. When he died, we got two small rescue dogs, both terrier mixes, and then I went off to college. Since then, it sucks, but my schedule doesn't allow for pets.

Same goes for exploring my surroundings, though I'm getting acquainted with the restaurants in my neighborhood. Take-out on the way home a couple of nights a week saves me from having to cook. I'm okay at it, but the menu is limited.

You cook?

Ross

Dutchford, Connecticut
Theresa
Life As We Know It

Who is this guy, and what did he do with the irascible, bossy man who'd been writing to me the past few months? Professionally, I've seen this type of behavioral shift when a person makes a major life change – in his case moving across the country to start a new job – and it has a way of shining light on alternate perspectives. People in these situations take stock of their lives and shift emotional directions. The thing is, I don't think that's the case with Ross. For reasons I don't know – believe me, I went back and re-read our letters, looking for anything between the lines to give me a clue – he made a decision about me, and opened up. This type of connection was what I'd been hoping for when I joined TLC. Now, I'm intrigued in a different way. Knowing how he first presented himself, and getting a peek of this man who's sharing some of his life in an easy, nonconfrontational way, I wonder what more there is to him, and how much he'll let me in. For my part, I'm happy to peel back a layer on the onion and share.

I've been sitting cross-legged on my sofa with my laptop propped in front of me on a couch pillow trying to compose my next letter in my head. I know I'm overthinking this, but I don't how to start. My phone chimes and I reached across Boo, who is lying beside the sofa, to get the cell off the coffee table. He lifts his head from his paws for a moment, decides the phone isn't worthy of his attention, and goes back to sleep. I see Max's name and tap the green button immediately.

Max is my first cousin on my father's side. Dad's brother is Max's father. They live in Northern California in the Anderson Valley – wine country. At eighteen, our *nonno* moved to California to escape Mussolini. Originally, our family is from the Monferrato region in Piemonte – huge Italian wine country and has been for centuries – and I have many distant cousins who still live there.

Young, determined, and too stupid to fear the undertaking he embarked on, *Nonno* decided he'd follow the family tradition and grow *Barbera* grapes.

In 1938 a person could buy a lot of land in the Anderson Valley. The population was sparse and *Nonno* hit it right. The highways didn't start to be laid through the county until after WWII, which meant with a little money and a lot of backbreaking work, he began to plant some of his two hundred acres with *Barbera* grapes.

For years, he kept sheep and sold the wool to ensure there was food on the table. He'd tried to join the army to fight Mussolini, but he was deaf in one ear, and they wouldn't take him. Their rejection turned out to be divine providence. His first harvest that produced saleable wine grapes was in 1945. Again, good timing. Wineries were buying up all the grapes they could get their hands on. The war was over, and people wanted to celebrate life.

What started out as a young man's adventure turned into a profitable vineyard, and in 1980 *Nonno*'s sons, my dad and Max's father, started Redwood Falls Winery. In 1992, when I was three years old, we moved clear across the country to Hartford, Connecticut, where my father had a job waiting in a food import company.

To this day no one but the brothers know what terrible thing happened to split up the family. No one talks about it, but everyone knew it broke my grandparents' hearts. I have no doubt that one of the reasons I became a therapist is rooted in the emotional fallout we'd lived with due to our familial schism.

As a peace offering – my sense is, though no one ever told me, it took years of negotiation – starting when my sister and I were twelve and nine respectively, we were put on a plane and were sent to California to spend our summers with our grandparents. By that time *Nonno* was seventy-eight years old. He lived another seven years, and our *nonna*, who was ten years his junior, followed him to the grave ten months after his death.

Those seven summers with my grandparents were magical. Until then, I hadn't known our family, most of whom lived in California. My sister Laura remembered them a little, but not enough to recall much about them. Such as our family resemblance, and how many mannerisms we shared as a family, and how deeply loved we were by people who hadn't seen us for years.

My mother's two brothers and their families, who live in Santa Rosa, came to the vineyard about six times a summer, and we got to know them and their kids. But since we stayed with our grandparents, my uncle Dominic's – my father's brother – children were always around. Mostly, we hung with them: Massima, who has always been called Max, Donna, and Luca.

Max is two years younger than me, but that never mattered. We clicked, and since that first summer, she's been my best friend.

Through the phone, Max breathed, "Oh my god," catastrophe lacing each word. No surprises there. Seven in the morning my time, four in California, and Max is not the type of girl to get up before the chickens. In fact, Max rarely gets up before eight-thirty.

"What's wrong?"

"Ziggy's knocked up." My mother's brother Stefano married a Norwegian, my aunt Asta. All their children have Norwegian names. At twenty, Ziggy, whose real name is Sigrid, is the youngest of their three kids.

"Lemme guess, she arrived on your doorstep –"

"An hour ago."

That explains Max's super early morning call. Ziggy has always been a bit of wild child and crashes regularly at Max's place. Even though Max isn't technically Ziggy's cousin, all sides of the family are intertwined in each other's lives.

My mother's brothers didn't abandon the Calapianos after "the breakup." They stayed tight with my grandparents, my Uncle Dominic and his family, and our family.

"She face-planted in my sofa a few minutes ago. Dead to the world."

I shook my head. "Hit me."

Max laughed. "Short version: she doesn't know who the father is."

"As in too many one-night stands having unprotected sex?"

"As in she's been dating two guys at the same time, neither knows about the other, and she's sleeping with both of them."

I sighed. "And having unprotected sex."

"So it would seem."

"It boggles. How pregnant is she?"

"About two months."

"Well," I slid into my professional voice, "if she's more than seven weeks along, she can have a DNA test done, but tell her fingernails and hair from a brush are not going to work. Both guys need to have a cheek swab done."

"You wanna tell her that 'cause she came in ranting and raving about how she was going to keep this secret from both of them."

"I'm guessing this means she's terminating the pregnancy."

"You'd think, but I'm wondering if she's opting for door number three."

"You can't mean going it alone?" The mere thought of Ziggy being a parent right now brought on unrelenting shudders. On her own with no help from the baby's father – double insane thinking.

"'Fraid so."

"So, the purpose of this call is not merely informational. You want me to shrink talk her."

"That's the plan."

"When has that ever worked?"

Max let out a long sigh. "Tell me about it."

"Call me when she wakes up. If I'm in session, I'll ring back as soon as I can."

"Got it. Talk later, cuz."

"Right. Bye, Max."

Ross,

Well my morning has been eventful. One cousin called about another cousin who's pregnant but doesn't know which of her two boyfriends – neither knows about the other – is the father. Apparently, she's been having unprotected sex with both of them. If you're shaking your head right now, trust me, I'm right there with you.

The pregnant cousin is twenty and not a mature twenty, she's more like a fifteen-year-old who's been let loose on the world for the first time. Right now, she is not mother material. Insult to injury, she doesn't want either guy to know about the pregnancy, and since she's passed out on our cousin's sofa, we don't know what baby mama intends to do. Frankly, I don't think she knows what she intends to do, but she has to make a decision soon.

I have a friend who has a great word for this type of situation: dramarama.

In Boo news, he has a terrible habit of eating anything he thinks smells good. When I take him for his walks, I try to keep a sharp eye, but he's sneaky. The problem is, he has a sensitive stomach, so guess who had to get up at three in the morning two days ago to clean up his mess and take him onto the patio so he could get the rest out where I could hose it down? Rhetorical question.

Cooking. A little hubris here – I can cook. I love to cook, and I've had good teachers. My mother is a wonderful cook, and both my grandmothers were amazing cooks. I'm 3/4 Italian. My Gramps – my mother's father – was of Scottish descent and he never weighed in on the food, except to compliment my grandmother. Aside from traditional Italian dishes, I enjoy cooking Asian food, especially Thai. It's all about the seasonings, and I admit to having a deep bench in my spice cabinet.

Actually, I'm a member of a cooking club of sorts. Once a month a member of this group of friends – all of us are foodies – cooks a dinner for the rest of us. We can cook whatever we want, but it has to be something none of us has ever cooked for the group before. Each of us has favorites, and a lot of us have traveled extensively, so the variety is vast and the food is always great.

Off to walk Boo before I head out to work.
Flower

Nine days later

Hey babe,

Yeah, I was shaking my head. Stating the obvious here – your cousin is fucked up, and so are those two dudes. Who goes ungloved? And who lets a guy go ungloved? Especially when they're not exclusive. Sounds like nothing good is going to come out of this.

Try carrying treats when you walk Boo. When he looks like he's spending too much time with his nose down in one place, get his attention and give him a treat. Eventually, he'll look to you for his walk snacks instead of scarfing the crap on the ground. Though, he's a dog and that's what they do. They're not what you'd call discriminate eaters.

You, on the other hand, are all kinds of discriminating when it comes to food. I'm not. I'll eat just about anything you put in front of

*me. I'm not afraid to try new things, but don't give me bird tongue
size portions. I need to feel satisfied when I walk away from a meal.*

Deep bench, huh? You into sports?

Ross

Max called when Ziggy woke up, and I talked to her – sort of. The
minute she heard my voice she went off on a tear, yelling at Max for
involving me, yelling at me for being "up my ass" about something I
know nothing about. My favorite passage of that non-conversation
is: "You even know what a condom feels like? Prob'ly not since you
get laid like once a decade. Lemme tell you what it feels like, Ter. It
feels like rubber over a dick. If I'm gonna get some dick, I want
dick, not rubber."

True, it's been a while since I'd had some "dick," but there were
legitimate extenuating circumstances that took me out of the dating
pool 'til recently. I'll get to that later. Prior to the lull in activity, I'd
had an active social life and a couple of meaningful relationships.
I'm thirty-one years old, and while I'm not wild, I enjoy men, and
I've had my fun. Safely. So I know, we are not living in the 1700s
when men used chemical-soaked linens as condoms.

I never got to tell Ziggy that she would still feel "dick" if the
man used a condom because she hung up on me. Max shared that
Ziggy stormed out two minutes after throwing Max's phone at her.
She hasn't heard from Ziggy since, and had tried to reach her
without success. I've been assured that if my crazy cousin doesn't
surface by this weekend, Max is pulling out the big guns and will tell
Ziggy's older brothers, Isak and Endre, that their sister has ghosted
and Max is worried about her.

Tactically, it's a better move to sic 'em on Ziggy without
knowing why she's disappeared. Those boys tend to be a little
extreme when it comes to their younger sister, and Max wants
everyone to avoid bloodshed and jail time.

Obviously, I concurred.

Ross,

*Your assessment has proved accurate. My baby mama cousin
didn't want our opinions or advice, isn't returning our calls, and
hasn't shown up at her usual haunts. She's done this before, but
typically she resurfaces after a week or so. We're concerned enough*

to tell her older brothers she's dropped out of sight. We're confident they'll find her.

Thanks for the treats suggestion. I've taken your advice, and so far so good. Though, you're right, it's in his nature to scavenge. Boo sure loves stinky smells. Sometimes he gets in full rolls before I can pull him up. He hasn't associated getting a bath, which he is not a fan of, with rolling in mess.

Spectator sports. I like tennis, but baseball is my thing. It's played in a park on a diamond when the weather is nice. It's rare for someone to get hurt, and it takes skill, patience, and quiet strategy. Plus, all those wacky hand signals from the third base coach are fun to try to decipher. I'm loyal to my team and have season tickets. I almost never miss a home game.

Non-spectator sports. Poker is my game. I don't play competitively, but I'm told I'm good enough to. I've sat a few high-stakes games. They were tense and exciting. I can see the allure of doing it competitively, but I don't have a cutthroat temperament, which is essential once you enter that level of play.

What about you?

Flower

Boston, Massachusetts
Ethan
Intuition

"Hey," someone calls as they walk by my desk. "Where are you, man?"

I swivel my chair to see Skip staring at me like I'd grown a second head. "Right here, brother. Whassup?"

"That's what I'm trying to find out. Something wrong?"

I give a quick headshake then, "Nope."

"Then why were you fifty thousand miles away? I must've said 'hey' three times before you looked up."

Shit. Flower on the brain. "Trying to piece together the best way to surveil the BU Russians."

He gives a quick nod. "That's why I came by. Team meeting with the ASAC in fifteen."

"Conference room?"

"Yeah." His chin aims to my iPad, indicating he wants me to bring my notes, then he heads toward his office.

I don't do *lost in thought* at work. Actually, I don't do it much, if at all. When I started The Letter Club thing, my intention had been to find someone to talk with who didn't drag on my time. Light, easy, make a friend, have a connection. It's hard to have female friends in general. It's even harder when you make your job your life.

Yeah, I know. That has to change. I spend too much time at work, where a small percentage of my colleagues are women – I don't do the hiring so give it a rest – and the nature of my job doesn't leave a lot of time to go for a beer after work. I have no time to meet someone I can hang with who doesn't have an interest in working my body, and vice versa.

Unexpected, and way too distracting, is this feeling of being drawn to a woman I can't talk to or see, but whose pull is undeniable. She writes things like "wacky hand signals" in the same letter she discloses she's a card shark. She has me dying to taste whatever food she'd cook for me, wishing I could hang on her back patio with her and Boo, and worrying about a fuckin' crazy cousin I *really* don't know.

Now, instead of rubbing one out in the shower before I go to sleep, I'm thirteen years old again, lying in bed with my hand on my dick imagining what she looks like – don't ask me how, I already know what she sounds like – while I go through all the ways I intend to enjoy her body.

I have to back burner her and get my mind in the game. The reason for this upcoming meeting has to mean we're in "go" mode, and there's no room for error with this shit.

Fifteen minutes later my ass is in a chair. My seven teammates, Skip, and the ASAC, a badass named Rashad Silverton, are all sitting around a large oblong conference table in a darkened, closed-door room. Rashad, at the far end of the table, has a laptop open and he's clicking through images that appear on the big screen behind him.

"This is what we have so far. No sign of the older guy Jonas described," a rendering of the guy flashed on the screen, "but these are a dozen of the Russian 'students' we've already identified." The candids on BU's campus were lined up against passport photos and images taken at Logan Airport's Terminal E. "We know for a fact three," larger passport photos of three men appeared on the screen, "of the twelve have entered the country under assumed names. Surely false identities were created to make a viable profile of an incoming or exchange student. We're firming up which, and all the information provided to BU. Based on these three," head nod toward the screen, "we are presuming most, if not all, of the 'students' Jonas said gather in his dorm are fictitious, and are affiliated with the Lebedevsky *Bratva* as are the three whose photos you see here." Fuck. Seriously bad dudes. "Their files have been sent to you."

Skip picks up the narrative. "We're in information gathering mode and there's a lot of ground to cover. When we're at a point where our analysts have gotten as much intel that's available on the suspects, we'll put our operation in play. Working up to that, you become experts on these people, their *Bratva* and their enemies. No holes, and no stone unturned."

Lots of questions and discussion ensued, then Rashad concluded the two-hour meeting with, "Stay sharp."

Hey babe,

A card shark, huh? How are you with tells, as in have any and can you spot them? My poker games have been friendly. The guys I've played with are about the same skill level, and no one takes the game too seriously. It's an excuse to eat junk food and drink beer while talking shit.

Can't say I've watched any tennis. Never played, but know it can be competitive. I like baseball. Good way to spend an afternoon in the sun eating hot dogs and drinking beer. See a theme here? My game of choice is football. I played in high school and college, defensive backfield – strong safety. Was never good enough for the pros, didn't even try out, but it allowed me to attend a good college on a partial scholarship, and that helped out my folks. Win-win. Since college I've been in the occasional game, usually around the holidays, and never full contact.

How's my man Boo? Any word on Ziggy?

Ross

While writing that letter I had to actually hold back from telling her about my day. I've never wanted to talk about my day with anyone but a colleague, and those recaps were more about work than any touchy-feely sharing. But today's briefing made me less happy than usual about the state of the world, and I would've liked to've unloaded on a sympathetic ear. Yeah, I don't have any hard evidence she'd give a shit, but something about the way she sounds makes me think she's really intuitive and would care. I'm pretty good at reading people – job skill, and I'm a watcher – so I'm guessing she's in the medical profession or a social worker, or something like that.

This particular infiltration by dangerous mobsters on my patch feels more personal. I'm sure it's because this shit impacts Jonas. Skip arranged for the boy to switch dorms. We don't know what's going to go down, but Skip wants his son far from it. If he were my son, I'd make him transfer colleges.

So far as we can tell, none of the Russians are in Jonas's classes. He's a sophomore, and apparently is a tech wiz, so his classes are more high level than a bunch of thugs could pull off. I've met the kid a few times, mostly when he was little and Skip worked out of the Portland office. Since I've been in Boston, I've seen Jonas once, and that's when he came in to help work up a likeness of the older guy who's the Russians' drop man.

Talk about all grown up, I have to admit, I thought the kid would stay scrawny, but he's taller than his dad, like six-two with broad shoulders and that surfer boy hair chicks love. He's still shy and down to earth. Good kid. I hate that this shit touched him even for a minute.

Even if Flower were really in my life, I couldn't give her any details about my job, but I could come home to her, tell her I had a crap day, and that I hate there are people in the world who suck big time. She'd listen, serve up a fantastic dinner, and after I'd fuck away my day in her arms.

Yeah, I've turned into a sap. But if I could live my dream with her, I wouldn't mind one fuckin' bit.

Ross,

Thanks for asking, Ziggy's fine. She came up for air after hearing her brothers were looking for her. We don't know where she was, but she banged on my cousin's door at 2:30 in the morning – seems middle of the night is Zig's preferred time to annoy people – went in and gave my cousin a ration for siccing the brothers on her. She says she's terminated the pregnancy, but who knows if she's telling the truth. It won't be long before we'll be able to see if she's lying. My guess, she's not. Even Zig knows becoming a mother right now would be a disastrous mistake.

Boo is doing well. He's settled into his routine and he's become quite a character. He watches my feet. No lie. He sits with his head down, or lies down and stares at my feet. He checks which shoes I have on and determines where all that fits into his world – are we going out or staying in. He knows the sounds of everything in the kitchen and how each sound pertains to him. Some bags I open, he doesn't budge. Others, he's right there knowing it's something I'm eating he wants, or it's something for him. He understands sit, stay, wait, gentle, and come. However, when he decides he doesn't want to come, usually when it's time to go to bed – he's crate trained – he plops his butt down and doesn't move. I'm not a fan of arguing for arguing's sake, and I have no problem with being in charge, so I get a leash, and the minute it's on, he trots ahead of me, and heads straight to bed. I'm of the mind he likes the production value of putting on the leash in the house. For reasons only he knows, it makes him happy.

The other day I was at the garden center looking for some new pots. A couple of my rose plants need more root space. So I'm standing and staring at the pots weighing the options. Some of the new lightweight plastic pots look great, like stone or marble, but I wondered about their sturdiness. So I took a couple down from the shelf – don't judge – and turned them upside down and sat on one, then the other. I thought the first wobbled, so I repeated the alternating sitting on each then decided maybe I should pull down a couple more to see if the model wobbled or if it was just that pot. Five pots were upside down and I'm sitting on each for at least a minute. Two green apron guys come by and watch me, then a third joins them. I'm waiting for them to ask what I'm doing, and when no one says anything, I announce, "Allow me to introduce myself. I'm Miss Muffet and I'm trying out new tuffets." All three of them nod and walk away. I laughed so hard I couldn't breathe. I bought two and they look spectacular.

Disclaimer: I'm a mental health professional – yes, a shrink – so this might sound a bit preachy. I can't say I dislike the game of football, but I'm not keen on the forced aggression in children. There are long-lasting psychological effects on young boys who are encouraged to be "tough." As the players get older the game gets rougher, and certainly at the professional level, there's a high rate of head injuries, which concerns me. Young men will have to live with the consequences of those injuries for the rest of their lives. I'm hoping you've never suffered a concussion, or worse, and if you have, I'm trusting you had proper medical care and continue to follow up with your doctor.

Flower

There it is. The pull. Why I have to meet this woman in person and make her mine. She thinks she's in charge, but her dog runs her. He likes to fuck with her, digs the leash, and she falls for it every time. She's a complete nut at the garden center. Staring off into space, turning pots upside down and sitting on them, and then thinking it's the guys who work there that are crazy when they nod and walked away. What did she think they were going to do after she told them she was checking out new tuffets? She's lucky they didn't call it in to have her 5150'd.

No surprise she's a shrink. They're all a little off. In her case, she's quirky, which works for me in a big way. I don't disagree with her about football, but there are a lot of sports that are dangerous. I've never understood why anyone would willingly jump out of a perfectly good airplane, or race down a snow-packed mountain on two skinny plastic sticks. The takeaway for me – she's a gentle soul, and given what I do for a living, I'll take all the gentle she wants to dish out.

Hey babe,

Didn't judge, but I sure as fuck laughed. Is it the garden center, or do you let it all hang out all the time?

Glad to hear Ziggy is okay. Someone needs to send her a warehouse-size box of condoms along with one of those pamphlets about safe sex. Yeah, I'm guessing you're going to tell me it'd be a waste of time and money, but no harm in trying. Hate to see her fuck up her life when what she's doing is preventable.

Yeah, Boo's a character. He got damn lucky you took him home. Now he's giving back the love, and I'm betting you're the one who thinks she's lucky.

I've been banged up from football, but never in the head. The worst injury was three bruised ribs in my junior year of college. A pileup and cleats can do damage. All healed, and no worse for the wear. Appreciate the concern, though.

When you say shrink, psychiatrist or psychologist? Not an easy job. Impressed you took it on. Do you have a specialty?

I'll save you the ask. I'm in law enforcement. Followed in my brother's footsteps and never looked back. Similar to your job, the work can be rewarding, but it's not easy. We both see the worst of human nature. The difference, you help bring people to a better place, and typically, I find them when they've gone too far down the road to get back to a better place. Not to say it's impossible, but I'm betting you have a higher success rate of getting them to turn the corner than the system I work in does.

I'm looking in my fridge and it's a sorry thing. I'm going to head around the corner to the neighborhood pub to get a cold one to go with my burger and fries. What'd you have for dinner?

Ross

Actually, the pub has decent food. Nothing fancy, about a dozen items on the menu, but they don't skimp on portion size and the fries are thick and crispy. Substitute comfort when I know there's something better, and I want that better.

The next morning, the moment I walk into the office, I feel it. The air is thick with tension, and Skip is coming straight at me like a fucking freight train.

"Conference room," he barks out. "Now."

I don't even bother taking off my jacket. I'm on his heels, and we're moving at a brisk clip. Rashad's inside pacing with his head down and his phone pressed against his ear. He glances up when he sees us and shakes his head at Skip.

"Fuck." Skip's hands ball into tight fists.

Within minutes the whole team is in the room and no one is sitting. While Rashad lays his phone on the conference room table, Skip closes the door.

Rashad launches right in. "Last night two female BU students were roofied. One collapsed where she stood, the other was dragged out of the nightclub where they'd been partying. Thank fuck the club has a bouncer on the door in the alley. He saw what was going down, grabbed one of the guys who turned around and clocked him, and then ran down the alley. The bouncer, yelling the whole time, went after the other two guys who had the girl by both arms. They were dragging her toward a car parked near the entrance to the alley. When the bouncer got close enough to wrap a hand around her arm, they dropped her, got in the car, and took off."

Rashad shakes his head, pulls in a deep breath, and looks around the room. Not one man has moved. Their bodies, like mine, are on alert as they wait for bad to turn worse.

"Both girls are at Mass Gen. The one from the alley, Sky Halpern, age nineteen, has contusions on her arms and legs, and she had to have a gash in her knee stitched up."

"Fuck."

"Goddamn it."

"Muthafuckas."

"She's gonna be at the hospital for a couple of days at least." Rashad looks around the room and I can feel the warning emanating off him. The briefing is about to go ballistic. "The one who collapsed in the club, Jessica Impertelli, age nineteen, had a heart attack and is in ICU."

"Those fuckers double dosed," I say at the same time the rest of the team looks like they want to kill someone, and fast.

"They double dosed," Rashad confirms.

"Cameras?"

"They have to have vid."

"The bouncer? He ID any of them?"

"These our guys?"

The questions come rapid fire and Rashad holds up one hand, palm out. "There's video, and it's being analyzed – too dark to see anything without enhancements. They knew where the cameras were and knocked out the exterior lighting, which the bouncer reported to his boss when he took up his post."

Skip says, "The bouncer gave a pretty good description of the guy who clocked him. When he'd grabbed him, the guy said something in a language the bouncer thinks is Russian. While he didn't get a good look at the other two, he did remember the car's make and model, and two numbers on the Massachusetts license plate. We're running all that now."

"In about ten minutes," all heads turn back to Rashad, "two members of the Boston PD who are on our joint terrorism task force will be joining us. We're going to bring them up to speed on what we have on the Lebedevsky *Bratva,* and the Russians at BU. From the likeness we've roughed out, it appears the bouncer described one of the guys from the BU dorm crew."

If I could've taken the temperature of the room at that moment, I'd bet we are near boiling.

"Read the police reports." Rustling sounds through the room as the team takes their seats and pull out their iPads. Fernando and Cam leave, probably to get their tablets. "They're comprehensive but evolving. Sky was able to give a preliminary statement and she remembers more than is usual in these types of cases."

Rashad stops talking and everyone is focused on him. "The Russian crew fucked up last night and tipped their hand. Now we know why they're here. Human trafficking is a big part of the Lebedevsky *Bratva*'s business. No doubt the guys who were involved will disappear. We need to get eyes on the remaining crew.

My guess, they've already decamped from BU, but they're not leaving. We're going to find these fuckers. They're not going to touch one more girl. You with me?"

Every head in the room nodded while every jaw muscle jumped in exceptionally determined faces.

Dutchford, Connecticut
Theresa
Go with the Feeling

My teeth hurt from the yummy sweetness of my *cafe sữa đá*. I took another sip while waiting for my friend Sofia in a small, unadorned, but traditional Vietnamese restaurant in Boston's Back Bay. One of my foodie friends recommended the place, and she was never wrong about great restaurants.

Remember the shifting characterization I mentioned when this tale began? Sofia is it. Initially, she was a patient. Circumstances changed when, during one of our sessions, her ex-boyfriend busted into my office and tried to shoot her. I took the bullet instead. After the shooting, she moved overseas for a few months. About a year ago, when she came back to Connecticut, we reconnected and became friends.

Our bond is unique and precious. Even though she understands it wasn't her fault, it took her a while to work past the guilt about what the ex had done. She's in a good place now, and in her I have a special person who will always be in my life who I can trust and love.

The bells tinkle over the door and I look up to see her walking toward me. Her face is glowing, her smile wide, and she has huge sunglasses resting on the top of her head, pushing her hair off her forehead. Her slender frame is draped in a scarf wrapped loosely around her neck about six times, worn over a denim jacket that covers a long flowy dress in multicolor geometric patterns. She's the picture of a lovely young woman channeling her inner artist.

I stand and move away from my chair, lean in, and hug her. "You look great," I murmur into her hair as she hugs me back. Two sparrows. We're the same height and body type – petite and small-boned, though I have ass and thighs, and Sofia doesn't. I step back and take her in. "Aren't you cold?" Late September in Boston means autumn is definitely in the air, and today is windy and cloudy.

She yanks up her dress to show me she's wearing bright red tights and clunky lace-up boots. "Fully kitted out."

I grab her hand and squeeze. "So British. Matteo's rubbing off on you."

Her cheeks pink. "Well, yeah." She smiles the smile of the besotted. "We're living together, even though my parents think I'm doing the whole dorm life thing. I mean, we leave the house early – he has to be at work at eight-thirty and I have classes that start at eight – and I live in my studio or in the library, and don't get home until after eight most nights. We eat, we talk, we...you know," she grins, "and bam, we're asleep to do it all over again the next day. So we're living together for about four hours a day."

"Sounds horrendous." I motion for her to sit as I retake my seat. "You look miserable. I'm worried."

She grins again. "I know. Right?" She looks at my drink. "What's that?"

"*Cafe sữa đá*. It's Vietnamese iced coffee made with condensed milk. Super sweet and fabulous. Their coffee is strong, like espresso."

"Yum. I'll have one of those. What do you recommend?"

I open the sizable menu and find many authentic dishes. Sofia has become an adventurous eater, so I pick two appetizers and two main courses. "To start, the crispy spring rolls, and shrimp paste on sugarcane. Then onto the *Kho To*, which is salmon *en casserole* cooked with caramelized peppercorn sauce and is topped with cilantro. It's a real treat, and let's have *Banh Hoi Tom Noung*, which is grilled shrimp they roll into rice vermicelli noodles right here at the table."

Sofia's staring with wide eyes. "You do this every time. I leave the restaurant so stuffed I can barely move."

I laugh. "Memory serves, no one pushes the food down your throat. You gobble it up."

She dips her chin.

"Anyway, this is light food. I ordered with your return to classes after lunch in mind."

The waiter comes over and I tell him what we want. After he walks away, Sofia asks, "I'm thrilled you're here, but you never told me why you're in Boston on a Thursday." Before I can answer she amends, "I mean, when you come it's usually for a play or a day at a museum and you stay the weekend and we meet for Sunday brunch."

I love this about her. She goes out of her way to make sure nothing she says can be construed as critical. Sweet down to her clunky boots. "One of my cooking club members is a Klezmer band that performs all over New England. They're part of a parade of performers at musical instruments convention, and she asked me if I wanted to see them. I said yes, and here I am."

"You foodies are into everything, aren't you?"

"We seem to be." I smiled as the waiter placed our appetizers on the table. "Dig in."

A couple of moments later all I hear is "mmm" and "wow" and "mmhmm."

"I'm guessing you like it."

She shakes her head. "No. I *love* it. How did I not know this stuff existed?"

I laugh.

"Hey," she asks, "no work today?"

"I saw three people this morning, one afternoon appointment cancelled, and I shuffled everyone else around."

"Cool. Playing hookey."

"In a manner of speaking, yeah, I am."

A few minutes later our main courses arrive, and I serve up half of each dish onto Sofia's plate. More "mmmm, wow," and "mmhmm" with a couple of "Oh my gods" thrown in. Sofia never met food she didn't like, and she takes in the world with unbridled gusto. This is a woman blossoming under the love and care of a man who looks at her like she hung the moon. I have to say, I wouldn't mind some of that for myself.

After shoveling in every last morsel, we're so full we can't move. Sofia is holding her belly, and I'm glad I'm not wearing my skintight jeans.

I, along with all of New England, heard or read the news last week about two college girls being roofied in a Boston nightclub. I have to ask. "Do you go out to clubs with your friends?"

"Nah." She shrugs. "Not my thing. Matt and I dance in the kitchen. He likes to slow dance."

"I bet he does."

She grins. Huge. "Why do you ask?"

"I heard about what happened to those young women and I wanted to make sure you're being safe."

Sofia puts her hand on the table palm up and wiggles her fingers. I take my cue and put my hand in hers. "I so love you. Thank you for worrying about me."

I smile and squeeze her hand. "I so love you too."

"You know what, though?" I don't answer, knowing she'll go on. "Amy was out with those girls that night."

My head jerks back. Amy is Sofia's best friend, and has been since they were little girls. I've met Amy at Di Caro family functions, and she's larger than life. If anything happened to her, Sofia would mourn for the rest of her life.

"Really? Is she all right?"

"The girls go to BU and Ames is friendly with one of them. Sky. Anyway, they're in a class together and hit it off. Sky likes to party, and the other girl is a friend of hers. They all went out together, but Amy had to get up early to work on a paper so she split about a half hour before Sky and her friend got doped. Ames didn't hear about it until the next day, then she freaked."

In my professional opinion, freaked is a damn appropriate reaction. "No doubt. Is she okay now?"

"Better. She comes over to eat with us a couple of times a week. Says it's the only real nutrition she gets. Anyway, she was over on Tuesday and she seems to be dealing. Sky went home. Her folks insisted she take a couple of weeks off." I would've made her transfer schools. "The other girl, I think her name is Jessica, she had a heart attack, and is still in the hospital, but she's out of ICU. I don't know how she's doing since Ames hasn't talked to Sky in a couple of days. I call Amy at least once a day, and I text her all day long. Matt told me to get her back over for dinner tomorrow night and make her stay the weekend. She agreed to dinner, but I don't know if she's going to stay. I'm working on her."

Sofia might be young, but she found a good man to be her life mate. Both of them are wonderful, decent people.

"I hope Amy takes you up on the offer."

"Me too, but she's stubborn, and says she doesn't want to be a cock blocker." I smile, and Sofia smiles back. "As if. Matt is not easy to deter. Trust me."

"I do," I say, chuckling.

She smiles. "Anyway, our room's on the other side of the apartment. If we want privacy, we can hang there."

"I'm banking on you convincing Amy to stay the weekend."

"I hope."

"Has the school offered counseling to anyone who wants it?"

"I don't know since I don't go to BU, but it makes sense. And before you tell me to tell Amy to talk to someone, I did already. Again, stubborn. But if I think she's bugging, I'll make her go."

"I know you will, Soph."

***

I'm glad I went to the hear music. It took my mind off those girls. My friend and her Klezmer band are amazing – passionate and accomplished. I appreciate their expertise, but I don't think I could listen to that music on a regular basis.

On the drive home, I couldn't shake the feeling that I want to talk to Ross about Amy and the whole incident at BU. He's in law enforcement, and, unfortunately, what happened to those girls happens all too frequently everywhere. Maybe he knows someone in Boston who can find out if that poor girl who had the heart attack is going to be all right.

I know, I know. I'm empathizing with another victim. But truly, what woman wouldn't? I remember that feeling of being in college: halfway between being a kid and an adult. Worries were limited to academic pressures and dating woes. Sure, there were assholes around, and my friends and I avoided them, and we were careful when we went out. But no one expects to have their drink spiked by a random predator.

Ten years after college, and four years after receiving my PhD, I still don't expect to be dragged out of a club half out of it because I've been drugged.

Ross "yelled" at me for sleeping on a commuter train. Now I know why. He gets what being a woman alone and vulnerable means in a sinister way. The things he must see and hear. I wonder if he sleeps at night.

I pull into the garage, click the door down, and sit there for a minute. I'm going to do it. I'm going to ask Ross about the girl who had the heart attack, but I'm not going to bring up Amy. That's too personal, and I don't want to share something Sofia told me in confidence.

After I dump my bag on the table in the front hallway, I let Boo out of his crate. Poor dude, he's been cooped up all day. Typically, I come home for lunch, take him out and play with him, and I make sure I go straight home after work, even if I have something on that evening, so Boo can eat his dinner, and he and I can have some time together.

For the first time since I've gotten him, when I take Boo out to do his thing, I'm wary. I live in a lovely townhouse in a quiet community. But tonight, I'm checking over my shoulder to make sure no one is lurking while I give Boo time to stretch his legs. After we come back in the house, I take my laptop outside and sit on my back patio – five-foot fence with a locked gate – to give Boo some more outside time.

Ross,

Good to know your football injuries were not major and have healed. I don't want to think of you hurting.

Last night I made falafel and tabbouleh. I didn't make the pita bread, tahini, or za'atar mix, but everything tasted good. I'm partial to Greek and Middle Eastern food, although I admit that there are few cuisines I don't like. Today, I met a friend for lunch at a superb Vietnamese restaurant. We were waddling when we left, but yum. The meal was spectacular.

I'm a psychologist with a focus on middle and late-stage adolescence. Most of my patients are kids in high school and college. As you can imagine, some of what I hear is heartbreaking. Not every outcome is Dr. Sean Maguire-esque, but I take comfort in any and all progress made, and hope I'm providing my patients with the tools they need to get them to acceptance and contentment. Happy is a great goal, but for some people it's not attainable.

Apparently, I let it all hang out everywhere. My inner goofball comes out in other places aside from the garden center, although, I confess, it's one of my favorite places to be. I'll share a fantasy – no, not any of those. And no, I'm not blushing. Here goes: I'd love to live in a house on a couple of acres of land where I can plant hundreds of different types of flowers, and flowering trees and bushes that would bloom as close to year-round as I can get. I'm not outdoorsy in the hiking on a trail kind of way, but I love being outdoors with my plants, and to have a huge garden filled with all that beauty would be amazing. I'd like to grow fruits and vegetables too. Makes sense since I love to cook. The idea of bringing in zucchini from my garden and cooking it for dinner that night would be fantastic.

Hey, I have a request. Absolutely, feel free to tell me no. I won't take offense, and I don't want you to do anything you feel uncomfortable doing or might put you in an awkward position. I heard about those two young women in Boston who were victims of Rohypnol spiking. I wondered if you could find out how the one who had the heart attack is doing. I know with all the things going on in the world to focus on this one incident seems unusual, but since I see patients who've had things like this happen to them, I guess I'm more sensitive to this story.

Again, if you can't or don't want to, no worries. Truly.
Flower

Boston, Massachusetts
Ethan
There Are No Coincidences

I couldn't fucking believe it. I read and re-read her letter at least ten times. What are the odds this woman would ask me about my case? I'm not falling down the paranoia rabbit hole. I don't think she's a plant. I know for a fact my home, car, and office aren't bugged, and my computer hasn't been hacked. The letters I compose and print out haven't been seen by anyone but me before I mail them out.

Do I think TLC might've fucked up and she knows who I am? Maybe. But the likelihood of that is not high. I'd put it in the ten percent range, and that's being generous. My gut tells me she doesn't have a clue who I am, where I live, and for which agency I work. I listen to my gut. It's kept me safe and alive for the past thirteen years.

I have to look at this rationally. The case made national news and she could've read about it online or heard about it on TV. If everything she's written is the truth, then she would be sensitive to these types of cases and she would be concerned about how Jessica is doing. But what set her off? There's something she's not saying.

She's held back before, particularly when I pushed her about what happened to her. *Jesus fuck.* I pray she doesn't share the same set of facts as Sky and Jessica. But, knowing the state of the world, it's sure as fuck a possibility. On average, there are about 300,000 incidents of rape and sexual assault each year in this country, and law enforcement knows these incidents are underreported. Most spiking occurs in alcoholic drinks, and around twelve percent of college students report their drinks have been spiked and they were victims of sexual assault. Those reports are made by the people who remember and who choose to share what happened. Most who remember don't report. The system sucks, and the victims know it.

I'm not a harmonic convergence type of guy. I don't believe the universe is talking to me, and if there is a God, I'm absolutely certain my shit is not on the top, middle, or even bottom of any list of things a deity would contemplate. But something brought Flower into my life, and now I have to figure out how to elicit information from her to determine where she lives. If I can get her to narrow that down, I will find her.

Hey babe,

Middle Eastern and Vietnamese. Damn. I'm jealous. I don't know that I'll cook any of that for myself, but there's a falafel joint not far from my job. I'm going there tomorrow to grab lunch, but no tabbouleh. Not a huge fan of herby dishes, or getting food stuck in my teeth. Yeah, some people brush their teeth at work. I'm not one of them.

I had to search for who Dr. Sean Maguire is and figured out he's a movie reference. Have to admit, never saw Good Will Hunting, but now I'm curious.

Well, Doc, you continue to impress. Of all the subgroups you could've worked with, that seems one of the most challenging. No wonder you take comfort in flowers, plants, and the garden center. Everyone has to find a way to keep their lid loose, and having a couple of acres filled with things you love sounds perfect. But why have flowers as close to year-round as possible?

I'll see if I can find out anything for you about the girl. No promises, but I'll try.

And, babe, putting a zucchini in the same letter with a fantasy has to be a subliminal message. You flirting with me, Doc?

Ross

Dutchford, Connecticut
Theresa
A Man in Uniform

Leave it to Ross to find a Freudian slip. Early on I'd guessed he's intuitive, now I'm sure. He understands my thing for flowers and gardening keeps my "lid loose," and he figured out I want to meet him. If the promise of him is half as good as I imagine, he's someone I'd enjoy spending time with. Don't hate on me for understating it. There's a lot to be said for finding a kindred spirit, but if there's no chemistry, no zing, we'll be good friends and nothing more. Not that such an outcome would be a bad thing, but seeing Sofia and the unbridled happiness she's living makes me yearn for some of my own. I don't know if Ross is that man. But I'd like the opportunity to find out.

Since he's moved across the country for his new job, he's either on my coastline or three thousand miles away. If he's anywhere on the eastern seaboard, no airport is more than a two-and-a-half-hour flight away. I'm not opposed to long-distance relationships, but if I'm in it, I want it close by. Maybe he's within driving distance. DC is too far, but NYC is doable.

Look at me, making mental plane reservations, and mapping out weekend road trips to meet a man who may be a complete sham.

But if he delivers on the status of Jessica's well-being – and he told me he'd try, which is something he could've blown off by saying he didn't know anyone in the Boston area, and I wouldn't know if he's telling the truth – then I'd know he's in law enforcement. Sure, he could be a complete nutjob cop wannabe, but I'd like to think I'd have gotten that vibe by now.

Only time would tell if he's for real.

In the meantime, Sofia had texted to let me know she'd convinced Amy to spend the weekend, and that made me feel better. Whether Amy understands what she's feeling is debatable. Most people who escape trauma have some type of survivor's guilt, but they don't tag it as such. Something like this might keep Amy from socializing in clubs or bars, which would be a shame since she's such a vibrant person. This week the other victim, Amy's friend Sky, returns to school, and seeing her will trigger deep emotions. Knowing that Sofia and Matt are looking out for Amy is comforting. From what Sofia has told me, she and Amy share pretty much everything. If Amy's having a hard time coping, Sofia will know and do what she must to get Amy the help she needs.

Hungry and wanting a quick fix, I'm staring into my fridge when the phone rings. I pick it up and see Max is calling.

"Yo, Ter," she sings in my ear.

"What's doing?"

"Guess who I saw at Henry's Wednesday night dancing her ass off in a tube dress that barely covered her ass."

Henry's, a typical small-town bar with live music, is a fixture in Redwood Falls. Given recent events, this call has to be about Ziggy. "Ziggy."

"Ding, ding, ding, ding. You get the grand prize."

"I'm guessing this means she's not preggers anymore."

Max sighed. "You guess right. That dress, which was more like a stretched-out scarf, left nothing to the imagination."

"Sounds about right for Ziggy. Did she talk to you?"

"Hell no. She took one look at me, curled her lip, and kept on dancing."

I shook my head. "Par for the course."

"Yeah. She's a pain in my ass."

Ziggy is a pain in everyone's ass. But I don't need to remind Max of that. She lives it.

"Hey. What were you doing at Henry's?" Max wasn't much of a drinker – another long story for another day – and didn't frequent bars.

"Remember I told you Lola's hubster Will got a promotion?"

Lola and Max have been friends since grade school, and Will started dating Lola when they were in the seventh grade. "Ah-huh."

"We were celebrating." She paused. "Well, Will and I were celebrating. Lola, who *is* preggers, and we're all thrilled about that, is nauseous all the time, so she stayed seated at our table and drank water while Will and I tore up the dance floor."

"I'd say sounds like fun, but the tone of your voice says differently."

"Can you give me a pass here? I'm trying to sort my head on some weighty shit, but I promise to share when I can talk about it without losing my mind."

Uh-oh. Max can be mercurial, and I'm being diplomatic here, but she works hard at keeping an even keel. She knows herself, her boundaries, and her limits. If she's unable to talk to me, which is never, a man is involved and he got too close. It's the only time Max loses her shit, and that hasn't happened for many years.

"Absolutely. I'm here when you're ready."

"I know you are, and I love you for it."

Geesh. She sounded so sad. If she couldn't handle talk advice, maybe location advice would work. "Love you too. A suggestion?"

"Shoot."

"Before your next day off, call Nom Nom Cakes and order two dozen cupcakes. Drive west, stop at Bodega Bay, get the cupcakes, then drive up to Jenner, and stay overnight at a rental. Walk on the beach. Stare at the ocean. Eat cupcakes. Repeat."

"You're a fuckin' genius. Thanks, cuz."

"Anytime, Max."

She hung up.

I lay the phone on the counter and hope she'll be okay. Then I decide to bake cupcakes.

While I'm whipping up the batter – lemon ginger – I wonder if Ross likes desserts and if he has a sweet tooth. Then I realize I've never gone out with a man who's in law enforcement or the military. No reason in particular, but I tend to like cerebral or artistic men who are invested in collaborative relationships. A few of them had strong personalities, and I like a man who challenges me, but I don't want to haggle over every little thing, and I sure as hell couldn't be with a man who thought he could tell me what to do.

Ross seems to have collaborative traits. He's caring and sounds like he's open to new things. He definitely has a strong personality, is overprotective, and is totally bossy.

Shit.

I've got Ross on the brain.

Ross,

How was the falafel place? I meant to tell you that I use Greek gigantes beans as well as chickpeas in my falafel. It gives them a greater depth of flavor. There are a few cultures that use a blend of beans to make their falafel. Which did you find?

I spoke with my cousin who saw a not pregnant Ziggy a few nights ago. Suffice it to say, Ziggy's still angry at us, and shared her displeasure with our cousin. That'll pass, and then a new drama will come up. Ziggy's cyclical. For the past five years, we've averaged a drama a quarter. Though we've had some banner years where once a month was happening. Unfortunately, we haven't had any quiet years.

After my cousin's call, cupcakes became imperative. Lemon ginger cake with caramel frosting. After I've had a couple – sometimes three, but that's rare – my craving is satisfied, and I give away the rest. Boo doesn't understand why he can't have the leftover cupcakes, or at least one. He hasn't grasped the concept "It's not good for you." According to Boo, if I'm cooking or baking, it's good for him.

I recommend you watch Good Will Hunting. It's a really good movie, and the acting is superb.

Almost year-round for flowers is not my choosing, but nature's edict. I live in the Northeast, and winter doesn't allow for flowering plants, trees, and bushes, especially when we have two feet of snow covering everything for weeks at a time. Conifers are lovely, but a pine cone is not a hydrangea.

Thank you for trying to learn how the girl is doing. I appreciate any effort you make regardless of the outcome. It would be good to know she's improving, but I'm guessing that's the case since, if things had gone bad, the media would've been all over it.

To answer your last question, what if I were?

Flower

Boston, Massachusetts
Ethan
What Are the Odds

Flower's letter lay on my kitchen counter, and it'd been there for two days. I haven't gotten to read it yet because two minutes after I came home and dropped the mail on the counter, my phone rang and I was on the move.

One of the members of the Boston PD on the Terrorism Task Force is a female sergeant named Benita. She has an Army background and has done two tours overseas. One in Afghanistan, the other in Iraq. One look at her and you know she's a badass through and through. She agreed to be a decoy and has been going out to area clubs almost every night with her "friend," another BPD officer, Shanisha, who usually works vice, but has been seconded to our team for this operation.

Benita's thirty-two but can pass for early twenties easily. Tall and lean, with long black hair, she's a looker, no doubt. Shanisha is twenty-eight and looks eighteen. Short, tight 'fro, huge eyes, and a body with more curves than a country road, she grew up in the projects and does not take shit from anybody.

Both women go into the clubs equipped with sophisticated technology. Body cams with audio are part of their clothing. Each woman agreed to be chipped with a locator. No fucking way is anybody going to take them, but we're being extra careful 'cause these guys are off their minds and don't give a shit who gets hurt as long as they deliver the goods. Doesn't seem to matter if the cargo is damaged in transit.

At each club we've placed four team members inside, always near the exits. Two team members are stationed in each of the three ordinary-looking cars we have parked around the club, each car equipped with blackout screening. From the outside it looks like no one is in the vehicle.

We've been at this for weeks. The women go clubbing five nights a week, our people are in place, and we're there until after the club closes. Then we do it again the next night. Everyone's on duty, pulling fourteen-hour shifts or longer, except the nights Benita and Shanisha aren't out in the clubs: Mondays and Tuesdays.

Last night we hit pay dirt.

One of the tactics the women use to lure these assholes is to leave one of them at the bar while the other "goes to the bathroom." The team always has eyes on the women, and when Shanisha left Benita alone, she was approached by two of the Russians, who placed themselves on either side of her, way too close for dudes talking to a girl.

The team reported that Benita had been approached, and Shanisha came back with one of our guys on her arm hollering to Benita, "Lookie what I got here, sugar. He's a live one." The Russians saw Fernando and took off.

Our guys tracked them out of the club and gave the make and model of their vehicle to our teams in the cars. We followed them to a residence in Melrose and sat on the house. Which is where I am now. Watching no fewer than eleven individuals come and go from the modest middle-class home.

We've been able to identify six of them as members of the Lebedevsky *Bratva*, and some of the guys who were in the dorm at BU. The other five we've ID'd by matching them to their passports. All five entered the country after the roofie incident. Who they really are is unknown at this time, but we're digging. We figure they're the replacements sent in after roofie-ing those two girls went bad. The three men involved in that clusterfuck are in the wind, probably sent elsewhere or called back to Russia.

Waiting sucks, but is often the most essential part of what we do while we build our case. We want to get as many of these POS as we can. We want to shut down the Lebedevsky *Bratva*'s human trafficking route. Personally – and I know I'm not alone in feeling this way – I'd like to beat the shit out of each of those motherfuckers. But right now, we don't have any of them engaging in criminal activity.

Two guys went to a club, chatted up a woman, then left. Six of them used to be enrolled at BU and lived or hung out in a dorm. NBD. Students drop out of college all the time. That they're from Russia isn't a crime. We checked, and all of them are here legally. We have no doubt those on the student visas will leave soon since their status has changed. Something simple as that to trace wouldn't go unnoticed, and these guys do not want to be on our radar. They'll leave and new men will come in. The continuous supply of members of the *Bratva* coming from Russia seems endless. Unless and until one of them tries to enter the country with a different passport than the first one they produced, we can't stop them from coming.

So we wait.

Adam – a team member and my partner in this operation – and I were relieved from our surveillance of the Melrose house at 20:00 hours.

I'm home now, and the first thing I do is grab Flower's letter, lie on the sofa, and tear open the envelope. Five minutes later, I'm in front of my laptop researching – like everyone else does – psychologists who specialize in middle and late-stage adolescence in the Northeast.

I can't believe she's that close to me. I also can't believe eleven states make up the Northeast. The total population of these eleven states is fifty-six million people.

The densest in the US.

Of course.

I grew up in a small town in central Oregon – population two thousand. I went to college in Eugene – population about one hundred seventy thousand. I worked in Portland, population about six hundred fifty-five thousand. While Boston proper isn't much bigger than Portland population wise, the Boston metro area is home to about five million people.

To say the odds of finding Flower fast are not good is a fucking understatement. *Shit.* New York State alone has over twelve thousand licensed psychologists. I'm nothing if not determined, but tonight I'm wiped. The past two days have been intense and I've had no sleep in nearly forty hours.

I take Flower's letter to bed and read it a couple more times. She's cute, and she's a tease.

Perfect.

With her on my mind, knowing she's no more than a few hundred miles away, I drop into a dreamless sleep.

Hey babe,

Too bad TLC won't let you send me cupcakes. I'm with Boo. Anything left over is mine. I like it all: cakes, pies, cookies, and pastries. I can't bake worth a damn, but my mom is a good cook and loves to bake. She had three guys in the house, and her mission was to make sure we were well fed. When we were teenagers, she used to tell my brother and I we were eating her out of house and home, but she made sure there were always cookies or a couple of pies around for us to dig into.

Think I covered the whole Ziggy situation already, but to underline it, she needs to calm the fuck down.

The falafel was good. Yours sounds better. When I go back, I'll find out where the folks that own the place are from. Somewhere in the Middle East, but I'm not sure which country.

Here's what I found out about the girl: she's home with her folks recovering, and she dropped out of college. I hope knowing she's doing better gives you some peace of mind.

I haven't had a chance to watch Good Will Hunting, but I will, and I'll let you know what I think.

Once you get your acreage, you should have a greenhouse so you can enjoy flowers year-round. My dad built an enormous greenhouse for my mom, and even though I'm not into gardening – too many years of having to pull weeds and mow the lawn – even I think her greenhouse is something else.

Now, about that flirting... You're good at it. Keep doing it.
Ross

What I can't tell Flower is that according to Jessica's cardiologist, while the prognosis about her heart is "cautiously optimistic," she may have suffered "mild cognitive function loss" due to the suppression of her heart at the onset of the overdose. In other words, too much time passed between the heart attack and when the EMTs got her on oxygen. Now, this bright young woman has to work with neurologists and therapists for who the fuck knows how long to see if she can recapture what her brain lost. I don't know the extent of it, but her speech is slurred, and she doesn't remember certain words. The good news is she's young, and the brain's amazing. I have to hold on to that every day to keep from doing something that will cost me my career and put me in Leavenworth for the rest of my life.

A VSD, Victim Services Division, member has been assigned to Jessica and her family, who live in a small town outside Pittsburgh.

We'll receive updates, but we've been told not to expect miracles, and that if there are improvements, they'll take time.

All this shit rolls around my brain as I'm stuck in this car surveilling the house in Melrose. Activity is sporadic. Some days, all eleven of these fucking assholes are there together, which we figure means they're plotting and planning. One of them must be the go-between for whoever's running this shit show and the soldiers on the ground. We haven't been able to establish who the "senior" man is, but everyone in that house is being followed.

So far, only the two who approached Benita are hitting the clubs. The rest are trolling the over one hundred college campuses in and around Boston. No surprise why they selected here. The pickings are ripe for their brand of human trafficking.

What we wouldn't give to have ears inside that house. But we know, and it sucks, the AUSA, Assistant US Attorney, assigned to our case told us she wouldn't even bother asking a judge for a "listening" warrant. The fact that the three guys who roofied Jessica and Sky have been seen with six of the men in that house falls far short of the legal threshold necessary for a warrant.

As a watcher, I don't mind stakeouts as much as other agents, but I have to admit, the work is tedious, and it takes a toll on the body. Sitting for long periods of time, especially for big guys who are used to working out regularly, causes serious muscle cramps. Peeing into Gatorade bottles – wider openings – is a necessity since we have to be as close to invisible as possible.

Staking out the house may be coming to an end. It looks like we caught a break. One of the homes across the street, and three houses down from the Russians, is a rental that will be vacated this weekend. We've secured the house, and we're moving in on Wednesday, the first of November. Adam and I are "the renters." We're posing as a married gay couple, which should make other men coming and going from the house less suspicious. Benita won't be at the rental for obvious reasons. She's following one of the guys who didn't approach her, and when she's in work attire, trust me, she looks nothing like she did that night.

I've got to pack up my clothes and Dopp kit. I won't be going back to my place until the surveillance is over. My bills and regular mail are being forwarded to a P.O. box in Cambridge. I'm not giving up Flower, and I changed my mailing address with TLC to a P.O. box in Saugus.

Another angle I'm working that may yield something is to talk to Natalia Surkis, who under an assumed name was hiding from a Providence mobster named Ivan Demko in Fiddler's Rest, my hometown. She worked with my mother, of all things, at Gusk's Hardware. Natalia approached me at a family dinner about her situation with Demko. At the time, I worked for Portland PD, assigned to the area FBI Terrorism Task Force. I passed the matter over to Skip, who was already in Boston, and he put together a case that resulted in Demko and his crew being incarcerated or deported, depending on their immigration status.

After clearing it with Rashad, who agrees that while the den of vipers Skip arrested and deported based on Natalia's information are Ukrainian, she might've heard names or saw the guys from the Lebedevsky *Bratva*. She grew up around Ivan Demko's family, and while mobsters were viciously territorial, she might know something without knowing she knows it.

Natalia, who is whip-smart, likable, and grateful I helped her, has stayed in touch. After moving to Boston, we've met for lunch a couple of times. People who work in law enforcement understand the value of maintaining convoluted or "questionable" relationships. Natalia Surkis fits that category with capital letters.

A senior at Brown University, she's engaged to the son of one of the most powerful Dons in the US. What did I say? Convoluted. Her fiancé, Gio, wants nothing to do with his father's world, and is studying to be a doctor.

Full disclosure: they're the happy couple who met through TLC.

Seems I don't have to reach out to her. I glance down at the screen of my vibrating phone and see her code – no names in my phone, which is going to have to be stored in my locker at work before Adam and I go undercover.

"Hey, Natalia."

Adam's brows go up.

"Hi, Ethan. How are you?"

"Weather's about the same as Portland, but less rain, so that's a plus."

"I take that to mean you're working too much and haven't sampled the great food, abundant women, and other entertainments Boston has to offer."

"Affirmative."

Natalia laughs. "Sorry to hear it." I grunt. "Listen, I'm going to be in Boston the weekend before Thanksgiving, Sofia's getting married."

"No shit."

"Yeah, unexpected, but Matt knocked her up, and since they're together, as in glued together, making it official is just a date change on the calendar."

"Everyone happy about this?"

"Everyone except who you'd expect to be pissed as fuck."

Now, I laugh. No way the Don would be happy his eighteen-year-old daughter is pregnant her first year at Tufts. "Yeah."

"So, the Sunday after the wedding, you want to meet for lunch before we head back to Providence?"

Manna from heaven. "Sounds good." I want to control where we meet so Adam and I can keep eyes on whether we've been followed. No way would I put Natalia in danger. Aside from the obvious, she's a friend, and my mother would kill me if anything happened to Natalia, could you imagine what the Don would do to me if his soon-to-be daughter-in-law got hurt because of me? "Since I'm the new local, I'll text you a place I've never been but want to try. That work?"

"Perfect. Can't wait to see you."

"Same."

She hung up.

I turn to Adam and say, "You and I, lover, have a date to meet Natalia Surkis and Gio Di Caro for lunch."

Adam busts out laughing.

Ross,

There must be something in the water, or the air. A friend called to invite me to her wedding. I knew she and her man were living together, and they planned to get married in a couple of years, but after she found out she's pregnant, the wedding has been moved up, by a lot. It's unexpected, for sure, but my friend will make an amazing mother even though she's young. She's the sweetest person

I know. Soul-deep good. And her man is a great guy. Their kid will have parents who adore each other, and will feel the same about their child.

I'm glad to hear the girl is home, and is with her family. Yes, it does give me peace of mind to know she's improving, and it was kind of you to do that for me. I'm going to keep a good thought for her full recovery.

No acreage yet, but I've been looking at greenhouses online for days...and nights. There are so many options, and now I'm into conservatories built onto houses in addition to having a greenhouse. Mentally, I'm spending money on a house I don't own, and a greenhouse in a backyard I don't have. Thanks for fueling my fantasy, although I have a feeling that wasn't what you had in mind. Unless you're into conservatories and greenhouses for alternate purposing. With that in mind, I'm going back to re-look at the available models of each and examine their floorplans in detail.

Flower

Holy shit. Flower did not write that letter and tell me she's going to Sofia Di Caro's wedding, and that she's thinking about us fucking on the floors of conservatories and greenhouses. Yeah, unbelievably, I think she did. On both counts.

Let's break this down.

I've established I don't believe in coincidences, and I weigh the odds in all situations. I've also been clear, I don't believe the universe absorbs billions of peoples' wants and desires, organizes them like a dating app or some version of a wish list, and then matches up who wants what and how they can have it.

On the other hand, if I'd never met Natalia Surkis, I'd have no connection to the Di Caros except as most law enforcement does: monitoring the Don as best we can since he's one slick motherfucker who doesn't leave messes.

I know there are random theories, and things happen based on processes that we can't predict. Like Natalia choosing Fiddler's Rest to hide in when there are tens of thousands of small towns in the US, never mind how many there are in the world. Then once she moved to Fiddler's Rest, she got a job working at Gusk's and became tight with my mother, who told Natalia everything about me. Which is why she approached me about Demko so she could get out from under to live her life with Gio Di Caro. Who she met through TLC. Jesus fuck. Connections in ways I could have never anticipated lined up and put Flower in my path.

I sat on my sofa, staring at my two duffles, getting ready to head to my "new" home in Melrose. Well, if the universe is in on this, it's having a giant laugh right now 'cause I'm going to be undercover for who knows how long, and now that I can find Flower, I can't.

Technically, I could, but I'd never bring danger to her doorstep.

Before I knew what I was doing, I opened my messenger bag and pulled out my laptop.

What she'd survived has been playing a loop in my head since we first started corresponding.

It didn't take but fifteen seconds to find what I had known in my gut for months now. After I typed in Sofia Di Caro, this came up:

THERAPIST SHOT TRYING TO SAVE PATIENT

Theresa Calapiano, a psychiatric social worker with a practice in East Willisford, Connecticut, was shot by eighteen-year-old Walter Randall yesterday at 11:53 a.m. Ms. Calapiano was in session with her patient, Sofia Di Caro, who was Mr. Randall's ex-girlfriend. Police have determined that Ms. Di Caro was Mr. Randall's intended target, but when Mr. Randall pointed his gun at Ms. Di Caro, Ms. Calapiano put herself between Mr. Randall and Ms. Di Caro at the moment the gun went off.

Ms. Calapiano suffered an injury to her chest, and doctors at Dutchford Memorial Hospital have said Ms. Calapiano is holding her own, but they wouldn't say more. Ms. Di Caro was uninjured and was released from Dutchford Memorial Hospital after undergoing a thorough examination. Ms. Di Caro is the oldest daughter of noted businessman Alessandro Di Caro, who couldn't be reached for comment.

CORRECTION: The paper regrets the error – Dr. Calapiano is a psychologist.

WALTER RANDALL ARRAIGNED TODAY

Eighteen-year-old Walter Randall was arraigned today for multiple charges including attempted murder. He is being held without bail in county jail. Theresa Calapiano has been removed from the critical condition list and has been upgraded to serious condition. Numerous attempts to contact the Di Caro family have resulted in this statement being issued by the family's attorney, Anthony Garibaldi:

The Di Caro family thanks you for your concern and well wishes. They, along with the entire community, are praying for Ms. Calapiano's swift recovery. The family asks you to please understand that they wish to comfort their daughter during this difficult time, and they hope that you respect their privacy to do so.

After the first sentence, I could barely stand, and stumbled to the sofa where I sat down hard. My Flower, Theresa, had been shot point blank in the chest saving Sofia Di Caro. I checked the date of the article and saw all this shit happened eighteen months ago.

I catalogued all of…Theresa's letters and realized she hadn't moved offices. She'd re-opened her practice when she had recovered enough to return to work. I've met a few truly brave people in my life, but I don't know if I've ever known anyone braver than her.

Secret Service agents are trained to put themselves in front of a bullet for the president, and other law enforcement have taken fire to protect civilians and government officials, but that's their jobs, what's expected of them in the line of duty.

Theresa's a psychologist, for fuck's sake. A gentle, caring woman who has dedicated her life to helping teenagers and young adults get their heads straight, some of them after horrendous things have been done to them. Christ, no wonder she wanted to know how Jessica was doing. Survivor empathy coupled with Sofia being in college in Boston…shit. Theresa must've been worried sick. True, at the time I hadn't known who she was, but now I hated myself for thinking anything negative about her inquiry.

I close my laptop and lay it on the floor, then lean back and drop my head against the sofa cushion and close my eyes. Bad move. Behind my lids every photo I've ever seen of a chest being blown open by a bullet flashes frame by frame in horrifying detail. Sitting up doesn't help. Everything in me is screaming to get in the car and drive to Connecticut. My heart and brain seem to have teamed up, and they keep telling me I need to stand guard and watch over my woman.

Okay, this is fucking crazy.

We've been writing letters. Only recently we've started to flirt. She has no idea who I am, where I live, or for what agency I work. Until fifteen minutes ago, I had an eleven-state area to recon to find her, like a fucking needle in a haystack.

Knowing what happened to her changes nothing.

Fucking hell. It changes everything.

But I can't do shit about it. Any of it. Not the shooting. Not her recovery. Not being there for her when she was struggling to put her life back together. Not putting that piece of shit who shot her behind bars. Not protecting her. Holding her. Not taking Boo out at night so she doesn't have to walk him in the dark. Not locking up the house before we go to sleep, making sure she feels safe every way I can make her feel that way.

Goddammit.

Unless I pull out of this investigation, I have to keep myself to myself.

As I'm pacing the apartment trying to sort through the ramifications of turning my life and career upside down for a woman I barely know, but want more than is rational, my "new" phone goes off. Adam. Or should I say Drew. I hate undercover names.

"What?" I bark into the phone.

"Are we having our first fight already?"

In spite of myself, I laugh. "No, man. Shit on my mind. What's up?"

"We need food. I'm helping the team bring in the furniture and shit. Stop at some supermarket and load up."

"I'm the domesticated one?"

"Man, you wear twelve-hundred-dollar boots. Yeah, you're the domesticated one."

He hung up and I stared at my boots, for which the entire team has given me shit since day one. Little do they know these are the old boots. I haven't broken in the new ones yet, and I'm leaving them in my closet in my apartment.

Right. Decision made. I can't pull out of the investigation, though I want to in a way that makes me ache not to. But the plan is set. We're moving in. Tomorrow we're being visible. We're having a couple of sofas delivered to sell the move, and keep us open to meeting the neighbors. We have new identities, credit cards, driver's licenses, gym memberships, photos of us together photoshopped against stock backgrounds from all over Europe. He's Drew and I'm Nick, and our last name is Mason. We own an online tech company together, and we work from home.

Everything is set to protect our covers, and to allow us to surveil those motherfuckers across the street.

After I sigh about ten times, I put the mail in a kitchen drawer, slide the laptop back into the messenger bag, sling it across my chest, then pull on my jacket, pick up the duffles, and head out.

On the way to Melrose, I pull an agency SUV, now registered in my new name, into the parking lot of a Stop and Shop and proceed to spend three hundred FBI dollars on food. I made sure to buy a couple of six-packs. We can't drink, but we have to keep at least some beer in the house in case neighbors drop by. I have my protein powder in one of the duffles, and I bought plenty of fruit and veggies.

Maybe I am the domesticated one.

Shit.

I want to go to Connecticut more than I've ever wanted to do anything in my life.

Dutchford, Connecticut
Theresa
Wedding Bells

Sofia is making her mother and *Nonna* crazy because they're making Sofia crazy. I know this because I hear about it three times a day. Another morning call is coming in, but today I've had enough, and I have a patient in an hour, so I'm putting my foot down.

"Hey, Ter. I know I'm being a pain in the ass, and I know you've explained this to me about ten thousand times, but I'm bugging, so let me have it again. Aside from me and Matt, there are going to be nine people at this wedding. Why are *Nonna* and my mother making such a fuss?"

I've tried sweet. I've tried guilt, and I've tried practical. Today, I'm trying dead honest. "Because you're the first one to get married, and because you're young and pregnant and they're worried about you."

Sofia starts sputtering to say something and I have to stop the oncoming tirade and calm that down *al momento*.

"Not that you're making a mistake," I rush to say. "They adore Matteo, and they know he'll be good to you. They're nervous because they want you to be happy. They're both women who've had or are in long marriages. They want that for you. They don't know how to express these feelings without hovering and trying to control every aspect of this wedding. They don't care if nine or nine hundred people are coming. It's all the same to them. They want to give you their love any way they can, and unfortunately, they're coming at you like tanks on a field of battle. I say, roll with it. Don't give on the dress, but if they want to you to have a makeup artist and a hair stylist, say yes. If they want to dictate the menu and fight with the restaurant, say yes. If they want to have Gio and Nat take me up to Boston in their car, I'm fine with that."

"This is one of the three million reasons I love you."

"Not to sound big-headed, but you've told me that already, and you're still freaking out. *A basta*. Let most of the things that are aggravating you go, and concentrate on you."

"I know." She sighs.

"Listen, I can't shrink them into calm. They are who they are, and you better than anyone know dramarama is the Di Caro women's stock-in-trade. Break the cycle, at least for this. You can carry on as usual for the holidays."

She's laughing. I take that as a good sign.

"Okaaay. They can have their way on everything but the dress and my headpiece."

"Excellent. Now, have you bought the dress and the headpiece?"

"No. But I could do that this weekend if you help me."

"Soph. Emotional blackmail? Really?"

"Puh-leeze."

Christ and all his apostles. "On one condition."

"What?"

She's supposed to say *anything you want, Ter*, but at this juncture, I'm not going to point that out. "Three hours. If you don't find what you're looking for in three hours, I'm out of there."

"It'll take fifteen minutes. I found the dress and the headpiece at Nordstrom. I just haven't bought them yet."

I'm not going to ask the obvious. I'm not. Yeah, I am. "Then why haven't you bought them yet?"

"Because I want you to see me in them first to tell me if they're all right."

I melt. This is the core of Sofia. She's eager to please, yet knows her mind. She's young, and this is how her inexperience expresses itself. In the years to come, she'll welcome my opinion, but she won't hinge her decisions on it. Right now, she's vulnerable and she needs someone who's not family to prop her up. I'm honored she looks to me for that.

"*Cara.* I'd be happy to."

"Thanks, Ter. Really."

"Here's a suggestion. Buy the dress and headpiece. I'll be up on Saturday, and we'll do the fashion show at your home. I'm sure I'll love it, and then we can go out to lunch."

"You know," her voice is thick with emotion, "you're the big sister I never had."

Yeah. Melting. "And you're the little sister I never had."

For a moment I heard nothing. Sofia must've muted the phone. Her hormones are all over the place and she cries about almost everything right now. She sounded watery when she comes back on and asks, "What time are you going to be here on Saturday?"

If I leave before nine, it should take me about an hour and a half to get to her house. "About ten-thirty. That work for you?"

"Perfect. I'll see you in a couple of days, Ter."

Sofia hangs up, and I want to call Matteo to tell him she's a mess, but I don't. She needs time to work through all this. Plus, she's pregnant. I don't know how that feels, but when my sister Laura was pregnant with her first kid, she was a mess. Talk about weepy phone calls.

Boo goes off, barking and twirling at the front door. The mailwoman has arrived, and the sound of the metal flap on the exterior mailbox going up then down is tantamount to sounding the alarm in Boo's world.

"You know," I tell Boo, "you do this every day, and every day nothing changes. Are you cottoning on yet?" He sits and looks at me with a tilted head with an expression that says, *you don't get it, Mom*. He's right. I don't. I wait until I'm sure the poor woman has left the stoop before opening the door.

Bills, bullshit, a notice from the garden center, Ross. I go to back to the kitchen, drop everything except the TLC envelope on the counter. Then I go over to the couch to savor his letter.

Hey babe,

If I didn't know biology, I'd agree, there's something floating around, and the people you know are catching it. But it sounds like this time, it's a good thing.

My brother has two kids, and before he got married, I would've sworn he'd never do that. After he got married, they traveled and had fun for a couple of years, and I thought, they're too into each other, they'll never have kids. When his wife became pregnant with their first kid, he became a wolf. He protected her like she was made of glass. And when their first child was born, he was wolf PLUS. He wasn't any different with the second pregnancy, and he's wolf PLUS PLUS now. He told me they're stopping at two kids, which I think is wise since I can't imagine him more protective than he is. What I'm saying is, it sounds like your friend will be fine.

I finally made it back to the falafel joint. They're Israeli, and the wife, who I had talk into Notes so I wouldn't fuck this up, told me they use chickpeas, garlic, cumin, crushed coriander seeds, salt, a touch of white pepper, and chopped parsley. She was happy I asked, and when I told her you used gigantes, she said they're tasty, but the traditional Israeli recipe doesn't add any other beans. She went on to explain, like I said, she was jazzed you were interested, she uses tahini paste, lemon juice, and garlic to make her tahini sauce, which is really tasty. I'm no connoisseur, but I figured you'd get what she was telling me.

And, just saying, you know you can put a rattan couch in the greenhouse. The floor's going be hard.

Ross

Shit. How am I supposed to go to work when he's sweet and sexy in the same letter? I decide I won't think about greenhouse floors or rattan couches until I get home tonight, have a glass a wine, and spend some time with my vibrator.

Ross,

While I'm waiting for my ride to my friend's wedding, I thought I'd bring you up to date.

Last weekend I played fashion consultant. If you're rolling your eyes right now, it's okay. I'm so happy for my friend, I'm a little gushy, so bear with me. My friend doesn't want a traditional wedding dress, so she bought a lovely ivory dress with delicate pink, blue, and yellow flowers (you know I love flowers) down part of the front and part of the back of the dress from a department store. It's off the shoulder with a scallop neckline and sleeves. I'm not doing it justice, but she looks magical in it.

To top off the outfit, she has a wide pearl and crystal (fake, but good fake) headband that looks like a crown it's that pretty. Of course, she has fancy shoes with crystals at the toes and really high heels, which she needs since she's tiny and her man is tall.

Got to go. My ride is here. I'll finish telling you everything when I get home.

Gio and Nat are wearing almost the same outfit I am: jeans, boots, and a sweater. My sweater is turtleneck, Gio's is vee-neck, and he has a bright white tee under it, and Nat's is a thick fisherman sweater that's slightly off the shoulder. She's such a knockout, she could wear a plastic garbage bag and look great.

"That it?" Gio asks, nodding at my garment bag and small rolling luggage.

"Yep."

"You have to be the only woman I know who travels light." There's wonder in his voice, and since I know his family, I'm not surprised.

"Hey." Nat smacks his arm. "I don't have much more than that."

"Much being the operative word in that sentence," he says, laughing.

She grins at him, and I swear you can feel their love. They're intense ALL THE TIME.

"Where's Boo?" Nat asks.

"Staying with his bestie, Sheena, a beagle poodle mix." Gio makes a face. "She's cute. Curly hair with beagle markings." He shakes his head like he doesn't believe that's cute. "She and her parents live three houses down, and we do this for each other when we're gone for a few days."

"Cool." Nat looks at Gio. "Let's go." She turns to me. "I can't wait to get to the Fairmont. We spent our first few days together there."

I grin. "Memorable."

"Ah, yeah." She smiles wide.

Gio picks up my garment bag and grabs the rolling luggage, then walks to the front door. "I'll wait in the car if you're going to do a detailed recap."

Nat chuckles and shakes her head. "He wants you to think he's embarrassed. Don't believe him."

These two are entertaining. "Onward." I wave at Nat to proceed me. "We have a wedding to get to."

***

The church is small and quiet, and the priest is nearly as old as God. But he has sharp eyes, and he recognizes the Don immediately. Not that Don Alessandro could sneak in anywhere if he wanted to, although I doubt he wants to – he's not a shy guy. He has four huge, tough-looking men following him into the sanctuary. They take up position standing at the back, their hands clasped in front of them. Sofia doesn't seem to notice them, which she wouldn't. She grew up with them around her all the time. She looks like a fairy standing next to her imposing father, who is gazing down at her with undisguised love.

Nat's snapping photos with her phone, and I want one of Sofia and her dad looking at her that way.

The Don juts out his elbow, and Sofia loops her left hand through to rest it on his forearm. In her right hand is a small, delicate bouquet of pink anemone surrounded by white baby's breath. As they make their way down the aisle there's no music, which is kind of nice. The hush is reverent and private, and it's as if we're let in on a secret – these people crazy love each other and we're the lucky ones to witness their union. When Sofia and her father are about halfway to where Matteo is, who's looking super gorgeous in a dark blue suit, crisp white shirt, and pink tie – you have to love him for matching the flowers – beaming at his bride, Gio and Nat move in to flank the priest. As she shifts out into the aisle, Nat hands off her phone to Amy, who seems prepared to become the official photographer.

One photo Sofia will frame and keep forever is a sweet, special moment in time Amy somehow caught. Sofia is looking up at her dad as he takes her hand from his arm and kisses the back of it, with, amazingly, tears in his eyes. When I hand the phone back to Amy for her to carry on, I see tears streaming down her cheeks. The emotion in the room sparkles with love, warmth, and caring.

Matteo moves forward, and the Don – to his credit, with grace – places Sofia's hand in Matteo's, and she hands off her bouquet to Nat.

The priest does his thing, gratefully for about fifteen minutes, Matteo and Sofia exchange rings, say "I do," and then Sofia goes up on tiptoe, throws her arms around his neck, and he laughs before laying a long kiss on her smiling lips.

The cavalcade heads to the restaurant, which is empty. Gio laughs as we pull up and says, "Apparently, it wasn't enough for us to have the private back room to ourselves."

Nat asks, somewhat rhetorically, "Are you surprised?"

"Nope," he answers, still laughing.

The four bodyguards take seats, one to a table, spread out in the front room, while we make our way to the stark white unadorned back room. A long double-wide table, dotted with vases holding pink anemone surrounded by white baby's breath, is laid with bright white linen. Over the linen is thick white butcher paper, on which sits plain white porcelain plates, wineglasses, water glasses, and heavy cutlery. Even if the aromas from the kitchen weren't wafting into the restaurant, from the old-school look of the place, I know this restaurant is all about the food, and I'm in for a treat. The real deal. Italian cooking like my *nonna*'s *nonna* used to make.

We start with a few bottles of *Rebuli Prosecco Cartizze*, and because we're a small group, everyone gets to stand up and make a toast. When it's Matteo's father's turn – the saddest-looking man I've ever seen trying to be happy – he hesitates in English, and the Don tells him in Italian to speak Italian. Which *Signore* Parisi does, and what he says is lovely. He praises Matteo's choice in marrying Sofia, and tells Matteo he's the best kind of son a man can have. Sofia tears up, and Matteo puts his arm around her slender shoulders and gives her an encouraging squeeze.

Only two people at the table don't speak Italian, Amy and Nat. Amy doesn't seem to mind, and is probably used to it given all the time she's spent in the Di Caro home. Some key words might have sunk in, but Amy seems to be going with the flow.

Nat, on the other hand, is wicked smart, and has probably half-learned the language already simply by being around Gio's family. I know I'm right when she too tears up at what *Signore* Parisi says.

After the formalities, the evening reverts to a noisy family dinner where everyone is talking over each other, conversations are being shouted across the table, and copious amounts of wine and astonishingly delicious food is consumed with the gusto of the starved.

When it's time for dessert, and I swear, I don't have room for one more crumb, Sofia is surprised when an exquisitely decorated three-tier wedding cake is rolled into the room. Edible pearls dot the swirls and rosettes of the crème-on-white frosting. The bride and groom at the top of the cake is the best replica of the real couple I've ever seen.

Sofia and Matteo stand and go over to the cake, and in old-fashioned tradition, he holds his hand over hers as she cuts into the cake. He plates the slice, and forks a small piece onto her tongue, then kisses each corner of her mouth. The room is silent as Sofia forks a piece into Matteo's mouth, then grabs him around the neck and pulls him down for a noisy kiss. We all clap, and Sofia's mother waves the couple back to the table and takes over cutting up the cake for everyone.

As I've witnessed more than a few times at their home, this really is another family dinner with the Di Caros.

After cake and espresso, Sofia and Matteo leave for their suite at the Fairmont, and the rest of us sit around drinking expensive brandy – the Don, Gio, and Signore Parisi – Campari and soda, only *Nonna*, or Limoncello – me, Amy, Nat, and *Donna* Di Caro. Aurora, being underage, sits sipping bubbly water as if she's drinking arsenic.

By the time we stagger outside – the Don doesn't stagger, and I'm certain that man has never been off his game for one moment of his life – one of the bodyguards is in the driver's seat of Gio's car, and the rest of the party pour into two huge blacked-out SUVs that I'd bet my townhouse are bulletproof. Which has me wondering if Gio's car is bulletproof. That's the alcohol talking. But still.

Gio's up front with the bodyguard, a guy named Tommy, and Nat and I are in the back.

"The best time…" Nat trails off as she pulls her long naturally blonde hair off her neck in a handheld ponytail.

"They're so sweet together," I say.

"He'd cross the Arctic barefoot for her," Nat slurs.

"Damn, Ace." Gio laughs.

"Well, he would," she insists.

"Right, baby."

Nat hurrumphs, then asks me, "You agree with me, don't you?"

I nod. "Absolutely."

"Ha," Nat shouts.

Gio is cracking up in the front seat. Even Tommy chuckles.

"You know what your problem is," Nat leans forward to ask Gio.

He turns his head and says, "I didn't know I have a problem, Ace."

"That's your problem," she shouts.

We're all laughing while Nat mutters, "He's not getting drunk sex tonight. I'll tell you that."

***

The next morning my head doesn't want to lift off the pillow. I crack open one eye, stretch out my arm toward the nightstand, and slap my hand around until I find my phone. I drag it to me and look at the time. Ten-thirty. Considering I fell into bed a little before two in the morning, not bad. I had a decent night's sleep. Now I have to convince my body of that and get it into the bathroom.

I'm supposed to join Nat and Gio in the lobby at noon. Nat's meeting some friend from Oregon who moved here a few months ago. Gio and I are letting them have some private time while we head back to the restaurant to pick up cannolis to take home.

Ten minutes later, I've successfully navigated my way into the beautifully appointed bathroom and dig through one of my little bags for Aleve. I forgot to take two before I went to bed and I'm paying for it now. I swallow two tablets and stick my face under the nozzle, slurping water to help get those pills down.

By eleven-thirty, I've taken a shower, the Aleve has kicked in, and I'm drinking a cup of coffee in the room, which is surprisingly good. Or it could be average, but I'm in such dire need of kick-starting my system, the coffee tastes like nectar from the gods.

After getting my jolt, I roll my luggage, with the garment bag thrown over it, into the elevator and make it to the lobby a few minutes before noon. I see Gio and tell him, "Give me a minute. I'm going to check out, then I'll be ready to go."

He smiles and shakes his head. "It's taken care of."

I look up at him to make sure I heard correctly. "I'm still a bit fuzzy. Did you say the room has been paid for?"

"In so many words, yeah."

I blink a few times. "You?"

He grins. "I would've if I had the bank, but no. Dad."

There's a history of me fighting with Don Alessandro about money. After the shooting, he insisted on paying every medical bill that wasn't covered by my insurance, including the rehabilitation facility, which I stayed in for three months past my insurance coverage, and then providing private physical and occupational therapists who came to my home for months after leaving rehab.

When I was still recovering at home and needed to go to doctors' appointments, he had one of his "men" drive me. He paid for moving my office, and removing all vestiges of the old office so I wouldn't have to deal with going back there and sorting through the mess. Then he paid for the first two years' rent on the new office, stating I needed time to build up my practice again.

My parents think he walks on water. My sister and brother-in-law told me I would be crazy to turn down the help. And, as you could imagine, I didn't win one argument with Alessandro Di Caro. As a matter of fact, I'm pretty sure no one wins any argument with Alessandro Di Caro. Except maybe Sofia.

"That's…that's…unexpected?"

Gio laughs. For a while. "You're part of the family." He put up his hand when I try to speak. "No. Really. Don't fight it. You'll exhaust yourself and get nowhere. It's his way, and believe me, it's his pleasure. If for no other reason than what you mean to Soph, you're in his heart."

"Loving Sofia is easy. I don't need his generosity to support that."

"I know that. You know that. Sofia and Matt know that. And Nat sure as fuck knows that. But it's his way."

"In other words, done deal, never to be negotiated."

Gio nodded. "Exactly."

Nat comes off the elevator carrying a laptop bag, her jacket thrown over her shoulder, took one look at my face, and says, "She knows he paid the bill."

Gio grins.

She turned to me and puts her hand on my arm. "It's annoying, I know. Some perspective. When I finished my last semester at school in Oregon, he came and got me in his private plane."

I feel my mouth make an O.

"He told me, I was his," she points to Gio, "and that was all the explanation I got."

"Right." I go to grab my luggage, but Gio beats me to it. "It seems it's an inherited trait."

"You better than most people know, pick your battles." I nod. "I can't recode his DNA," she shoots a glance at Gio, "so," she shrugs, "I don't fight what I can't win."

"Smart woman," I tell her.

"Practical," she replies.

After we're settled in the car – Nat's in the back since she's going to meet her friend, and we're joining up with them later – Gio asks, "Where to?"

"Monument Restaurant and Tavern," Nat says. She gives him the address and we're there in less than fifteen minutes. She leans forward and Gio turns his head. They kiss, and she says, "See you in a bit." Then she leaves the car, and Gio and I head off to get cannolis.

Boston, Massachusetts
Ethan
Tilt

Adam and I arrive at Monument Restaurant and Tavern at the appointed time: twelve forty-five. I'm jumpy as fuck, and I can't let that shit see the light of day. Natalia knows Theresa. Saw her yesterday at the wedding. They probably see each other more than occasionally since they have Sofia in common. I feel like a kid in junior high wanting to ask a friend of the girl who I want to meet to tell me if she likes me, and will she talk to me by my locker. Not that I ever did that shit, but you get me.

We walk into the restaurant and I scan left to the seating area in front of the open kitchen, then right, where against the far wall the bar runs almost the length of the place. Natalia is sitting by herself, her head down, probably looking at her phone. She's at a four-top to the left of the bar, as I'd requested when I made the reservation.

I chose this place because it's in a busy neighborhood, and anyone following Drew and Nick would see they went into Boston for brunch at a trendy place. More to the point, the walls are brick and are about twenty feet high. There are few windows, and most of them are placed way up on the wall. Adam and I can keep a three-sixty on the place from the reserved table's vantage point, and the four-tops are made of thick wood, useful if we need them for cover.

Natalia turns her head, and when she sees me, she moves off her chair, sticks her phone in her back pocket, comes out into the aisle, and gives me a hug. I reciprocate, look down to her seriously pretty face, and ask, "Where's Gio?"

"He went to the North End to buy cannolis to bring home."

"Ah."

"He'll be here in about a half hour. Who's your friend?"

Adam's eyes are bright, and it looks like he's trying not to pounce on Natalia like she's his next meal.

"Sorry," I say. "This is my partner, Adam Gydansky." Adam pulls himself together, leans in, and shakes her hand.

"Nice to meet you." She flips her long blonde hair over her shoulder. "Your people are from the northern peninsulas, huh?"

He shoots me a quick glance, and I grin. "Told you she's whip-sharp."

She motions to the table, and we sit, Adam and I with our backs to rear of the restaurant. "Thanks for the compliment, but as you know, I made it my business to learn all I could about the states and countries in the former Soviet Union." She stares at Adam for a long moment. "I'm guessing you've been told why."

"Yes, ma'am."

"Natalia. Ma'am puts me over fifty and I've got a ways to go to hit that number."

"Forgive me," he says in Russian.

"No problem," she answers in Russian.

Adam turns his head to me. "She's an asset." Then to her, he asks, "What can we do to lure you into our world?"

"Great offer, but I'm not cut out for bureaucracies. I'm independent. I share my opinions freely. I don't have the patience or inclination to work for anyone who isn't as smart as I am. I can make more bank in the tech world, and do it mostly working from home."

"Shame," Adam mutters.

"But I get to play with you guys from time to time." She lifts her brows. "Like today, I'm presuming, since Ethan brought his plus one."

Adam and I laugh. She has no idea how apt her description is given our undercover personas.

I pull out my phone, bring up the photos I want her to look at, and then push the cell across to her. "Scroll through and tell me if you recognize any of these guys."

She takes her time, using her fingers to enlarge the faces, and examines each for a while. When she gets through with the last picture, she goes back one and she enlarges the face again, and then taps on the phone. "Him," she mumbles as if she's talking to herself. She tilts her head and closes her eyes. After a few long moments, she opens them, looks at the photo again, and says, "V." She closes her eyes again and shakes her head. "Vassily. No. That's not right. Vitali. Vitali. Nope." More finger tapping on the picture. "Viktor. Yeah, yeah. It's Viktor. I'm not sure of the last name. I think it ends in renko. Something like Urenko, but don't make me swear to that. But Viktor is his first name." She nods. "I saw him about six years ago. He was younger and skinnier, and he had a mustache. He was arguing with Vasyl, and Vasyl kept yelling in Ukranian, 'Viktor, you idiot. We can't do that.' Only one time, Vasyl said Viktor's last name, which is why it's not sticking. I have no idea what they were fighting about. I think Viktor came back once, maybe twice. I remember one time when he was in the house when I came home from school. I ran upstairs right away." She sits back. "That's it. That's all I remember. I don't know the rest of them."

Jesus fuck. Adam's right, and I knew this going in: she's a huge asset. The guy she pointed out is not one of the six who were in the BU dorm, and his passport does not ID him as Viktor Urenko or any name close to that.

We stop talking as a waitress stops at the table. We place our drink order, and Natalia pushes the phone back to me.

I lower my voice and ask, "Did Vasyl speak Russian?"

"Yeah. They all did. There were no borders, no loyalty to country, no national pride. It was all about the money, and the Russians have more of it. The Demkos wanted in on that."

With every word she speaks my mind is racing. We have to widen the net and bring other field offices into the investigation. My guess, we're duplicating efforts, and a lot of these cells are linked, which means we need to coordinate. Shit. If it hadn't been for Jonas, we wouldn't have "stumbled" upon these fuckwads. In my gut, I know we're barely scratching the tip of the iceberg,

"One last thing," I say.

"Shoot," she replies.

I drop my voice to a whisper. "You ever hear of the Lebedevsky *Bratva?*"

She sits back and looks at the ceiling, then shakes her head. "Sorry, doesn't ring a bell." She stops and squints. "But…sometimes Vasyl and Ivan talked about *bratva*s, but I don't remember any specific names."

Adam leans in and says, "Thank you. You're given us a lot to work with."

"Glad to help." She smiles.

The waitress puts our drinks in front of us, and as I'm taking a gulp of my ginger ale, Gio walks in with a beautiful, petite woman by his side. I nearly choke as I put down my glass. As they approach the table, they're talking, and she's animated, her long dark hair swinging past her shoulders and seems like it goes halfway down her back. She looks up at him while saying something that makes him laugh.

And I know.

Down to my soul.

That's her.

My Theresa.

My mouth goes dry, my palms start sweating, and my heart is thundering in my ears.

I can't stop looking at her, and I want to jump up, gather her in my arms and kiss her until the sun leaves the sky.

She's fucking perfect from her kickass boots to the waves in her thick dark brown hair.

Natalia must've caught me staring and turns around. When she sees Gio, she gets up and steps in the aisle. He walks right to her, wraps her up in his arms, and they kiss like they haven't seen each other in days. When he lifts his head, he smiles down at her, then looks over to me and Adam.

"Hey, man." He puts out his hand and it takes a moment for me to remember what to do. I shake and he calls, "Hey," to Adam.

I open my mouth to speak, but nothing comes out. Theresa has sidled up to the table and is standing inches away from me. She's surprised, and she's looking at me like she knows who I am.

Adam sticks out his hand to Gio. "I'm Adam."

Finally, I find my voice, but barely, her floral – of course – scent is permeating my brain and it's difficult to string two sentences together. "Adam's my partner."

"At the FBI," Natalia throws in fast as she glances at Theresa, whose cupid's bow lips form a small O at that information.

Natalia's taking us in, and smart as she is, she misses nothing. "Ethan, Adam, this is a dear family friend, Theresa Calapiano." Theresa waves to us, and it's fucking cute. Usually, I don't do cute, but it's Theresa, so it's fantastic. "Theresa, our friend Ethan, and our new friend, Adam."

She sticks out her small hand and reaches her arm across the table to Adam, who wraps his big paw around her delicate fingers. I get ready to smack him if he's not gentle, and as if he senses my thoughts, lightly, he squeezes her fingers. "Pleasure to meet you," she says in the exact husky, sultry voice I've heard in my head for months, and now feel in my dick.

He nods his greeting, and I stand up.

"I'm Ethan Berenikoff." I hold out my hand to her and pray I don't do something stupid when she touches me. Her hand is light and warm in my palm, and without thought, I turn my hand and twine her fingers with mine. "Here." I guide her to my seat. "Please sit. I'll get another chair."

After she's seated, she continues to clasp my hand, and the moment is frozen in time. Gio, Adam, and Natalia seem to be holding their breath, and while I know they're watching us, all I can see, feel, and smell is Theresa. Her piercing golden-brown eyes are captivating, and I don't want to tear my gaze away from her sweet face.

"The chair," I manage to rasp out.

"Of course," she says as she releases my fingers and puts her hand in her lap.

At the loss of her touch, I feel like a part of me has been ripped away. I nearly trip myself up when I turn to look at the other tables to see if there's an empty chair. A four-top a couple of tables up has three people. I force one foot in front of the other to head over to them to ask them for the chair.

As I'm walking away, I hear Theresa say, "He's the one from Oregon, right?"

Somehow, my intuitive Flower has figured out I'm her Ross.

***

"Oh my god, she didn't." Theresa is laughing and her amazing eyes are dancing as Natalia continues telling tales about my mother's matchmaking escapades.

"Honest. Every time Ethan came home to visit, Mrs. B had another willing victim—"

"Hey now," I warn.

Natalia smiles and says, "Single woman," then coughs like something's stuck in her throat, "at the dinner table. Then, after months of Ethan politely telling each woman 'Nice to meet you,' Mrs. B decides he must be gay," Adam barks out a laugh only I fully understand, "and starts inviting single men over to join them for dinner every time Ethan came home."

Theresa's slapping the table, her hand inches from mine, barely missing hitting my plate with each smack. She's laughing so hard there are tears forming in the corner of her eyes.

"After the second guy, right?" I nod at Natalia to confirm she remembers events correctly. "Ethan stopped coming home to visit for a couple of months."

As Theresa dabs her eyes with a napkin, she says, "God, that's funny." She looks at me with a wide smile. "Your mother's a character, huh?"

"My mother is an undeterred force of nature."

"Sounds like *Nonna*," Gio says from behind his hand. He has a mouthful of French fries.

"Mrs. B takes a gentler approach," Natalia says. "But the effect is the same."

Adam lifts his chin and says, "We gotta get back."

I nod.

The thought of leaving Theresa has me reconsidering my profession. I want to follow her back to Connecticut and build her a conservatory and a greenhouse. There's so much to say, and there's no time to go deep. And I'm not having a conversation with her unless it's private.

We can't take a walk in the nearby park. We can't leave here together period. So far – and I know Adam's been scanning as much as I have – there's no indication we've been followed. But if I'm seen with Theresa, I might as well draw a target on her forehead, and that's not fucking happening.

"Gimme a minute," I tell everyone. "I'll be right back."

I walk through the opening at the back of the restaurant that leads to the bathrooms. There's a short hallway, and the bathrooms are to the left, but there's a door at the end of the hall to the right. I walk to it, try the handle and find it's locked. Then I turn, walk back out into the restaurant and go to the end of the bar. I lift my chin to get the bartenders' attention. While one of the guys is walking toward me, I stick my hand in my front pocket and pull out a couple of Grants.

When the bartender is right in front of me, I slide the bills to him, angle my head toward the hall, and ask, "That a storeroom back there?"

The bartender nods.

"Mind if I use it for about ten minutes? Need to talk to my woman in private."

His brows go up.

"Not that, man. Really, talking, that's it."

He slides the bills into his hand and jams them into his front pocket, then walks toward the middle of the bar, opens a drawer under the lip of the wooden counter, and comes back with a key he slides to me.

I lift my chin and say, "Ten minutes."

As I'm moving to our table, Natalia's gaze is on me, and her lips are fighting a smile. I shake my head, and she grins.

Theresa looks up as I'm about to lean down. I give her a blink of acknowledgment, dip in, and whisper in her ear, "Let's talk." I draw back and she nods. To the group, I say, "We'll be back." I catch everyone's knowing looks and don't fucking care.

I help Theresa off her chair, and she takes my hand, threading her fingers through mine, which hits me in my dick and my heart. I love that she made the first move. Since she sat down at our table, she's given every indication she's as into me as I'm into her.

When we get to the back hallway, I pull the key out of my pocket and let us into the storeroom. I hit the light switch and two hanging fluorescent fixtures zap on, barely illuminating large shelves filled with paper towels, toilet paper, liquid soap, cases of liquor, salt, pepper, mustard, and ketchup, and there are dish towels wrapped in bundles stacked nearly to the ceiling. It's musty with the stench of old cardboard and industrial cleaner, which must be on the other side of the stacks.

"Sorry, it's not the Ritz, but I wanted somewhere we could talk in private."

Before "private" is all the way out of my mouth, she grabs the material below the collar of my button-down and pulls, forcing my upper body to lean down as she comes up and places her soft lips to mine. No further encouragement is needed. I wrap her in my arms and pull her up and flush with my body as my tongue spears into her warm, wet, ambrosia-filled mouth.

Holy shit. Tiny Theresa is a tigress, giving and taking right along with me. She moans, I growl, we cling, and swear to God, I'm about to come in my pants. Gently, I pull back, but I don't release her as I try to get my breathing under control.

She grins. "Hey, Ross."

"Wassup, Flower?"

"I knew it was you the moment I saw you." She lays her little hand on my face and looks me in the eye. "You?"

I shake my head, and her hand slides down to my chest where it feels great. Right. Like it belongs there. "Natalia called to invite me to lunch, and told me she was going to be in Boston because Sofia's getting married. When I got your letter, the facts were too aligned to miss you were talking about the same wedding. I did a search to find out who you are."

"Hmm. Cop brain." She touched her chest, and I figured it's an unconscious gesture. Christ. Her scar probably still hurt. "Did you know I'd be here today?"

"No. Thought I was having lunch with Natalia and Gio." I put my hand over hers where it rested near my heart. "The article didn't have a photo, but I knew it was you when you walked in with Gio. No doubt in my mind."

"This should be weird," she mutters.

"Fuck, no it shouldn't. I've told you more about me, straight on or inadvertently, than I've told anyone outside my family."

She nods. "Writing is intimate in a way I didn't expect." She sighs and presses into my chest. "What now?"

"Timing sucks." I feel myself tensing up, and she must sense it because she gets even closer. "I just started an undercover op, and no fuckin' way are you going to be seen with me until these motherfuckers are arrested and behind bars with no chance of bail."

"You're looking into the people who hurt those girls."

"You know, this intuitiveness can be a bit unnerving."

She grins. "It's an advantage I enjoy having."

"I bet." I give her a brief squeeze. "Can't talk about the case, and I couldn't tell you more than I have about…the girl, but know that I want those fuckers' heads on a platter."

"I'm sure I speak for all women when I say, no more than we do."

I nod. "No doubt."

"So?" she asks.

"So, we keep writing and stay Flower and Ross. Don't ask about anything that gives any indication you know who I am, and I'll do the same. But, please, write. Tell me about your crazy cousins, your friends, Boo, your plants, which greenhouse and conservatory you want, where you want to live, the garden center...all of it."

"Someone's been paying attention."

"Woman." I shake her gently. "If I wasn't on this op, where do you think we'd be right now?"

Her smile is bright, wide, and full of teeth.

"Right. And where do you think this is going?"

"Too soon to start mapping towns that are at the midpoint between Dutchford and Boston?"

Fuck no. She's been under my skin for months, and I've been aching to meet her, be with her. Now that I know the fantasy doesn't do justice to the reality, I'm not wasting any time. I'm thirty-four years old and I know what I want, and she's standing right here in my arms.

I shake my head.

"Okay," she says.

"Glad we got that straightened out."

She lays her head against my chest. "You have to go."

I cup the back of her head and run my fingers through her thick, soft hair. "I hate it, but yeah, I gotta go."

She turns her head, looks me in the eye, and stretches up, probably on her tiptoes, then whispers, "More."

Fuck the tiptoes, I grab her ass, which is superb. Round and juicy. My dick is so hard, I could nail two by fours together with it.

I haul her up my body, and she wraps her legs around my torso, and we lay waste to each other's mouths.

When I'm sure I'm a minute away from coming in my jeans, I pull back and rest my forehead against hers.

She runs her fingers over my mustache, then through my beard. "I thought you guys are supposed to be clean shaven."

"Joint terrorism task force," I rasp out. "Sometimes you have to look the part."

"Berenikoff," she whispers into my neck. "Russians."

"Yeah," I whisper back into the hair at her temple. This is killing me. "I don't know how long this is going to take, babe."

"Lots to look forward to."

"Hell yeah."

I jiggle her and she releases her legs, and slowly slides down my body.

"Not that I think there's any reason for you to be concerned, but if you see or hear anything that's suspicious or even gives you pause, you call nine-one-one. Then you call Rashad Silverton, our assistant special agent in charge, or Skip Vandenberg, our supervisory special agent. I'll give you their numbers before you leave, and I'll let both of them know who you are so they'll take the call."

She nods. "Okay."

I bend down and touch my lips to hers.

"Stay safe," she whispers.

"Got to, babe. I have a greenhouse to build."

She smiles, twines her fingers through mine, and we leave the storeroom.

***

After I add Rashad and Skip's numbers into her phone, Adam and I say our good-byes to Gio and Natalia, and I give Theresa one last hug. I don't want to let go. She reaches down and squeezes my hand, then she walks out, threading her arm through Natalia's.

Adam and I watch them leave, and we wait for five minutes before we go.

Once in the car, Adam says, "Seems like that was the first time you met in person."

"Yeah. We've been getting to know each other…long distance."

"She's way into you."

I grin. "That works since I'm way into her."

"Happy for you, man."

"Be happier once we put these motherfuckers down so I can get on with my life."

Gio's Car – Heading Back to Dutchford
Theresa
Refraction

Physics isn't my specialty, but I enjoyed studying it in college. One thing that has stuck with me over the years is, when there's a change in direction of a wave passing from one medium to another caused by its change in speed, that's called refraction.

Everything I am, and everything I will be, has changed. It feels as if for years I've been driving in mud and suddenly I hit clean road, and my trajectory alters irrevocably. I'm moving faster. Steadier. With more purpose, and a clear direction.

Although physically I can't be refracted, the concept applies.

Prior to getting shot in the chest, I had a great life. A full calendar of patients. Respect in my professional community. Friends. The occasional lover. I went out. I dated. I had fun. I knew someday I'd find someone who I'd want to spend my life with, and we'd get married and have a family. I like the tradition, and want that for myself.

I didn't "find" someone. Simultaneously, we became attached to each other in a way I know, we'll never get unstuck.

Ethan Berenikoff didn't slowly work his way into my life. He crash-landed into it. True, we've been writing for a while and over time I went from looking forward to his letters to craving them. And sure, I've fantasized what it would be like to meet him. Spend time with him. Fuck his brains out. But actually meeting him, laughing with him, touching him, kissing him, feeling his massive erection pressing against my body not only changed my direction, it changed my speed.

Now, patience has flown out the window, and I can't wait for him to get those bastards who hurt those girls, and be done with his undercover assignment so we can get busy doing e-v-e-r-y-t-h-i-n-g. Slowly.

I want to…no, need to spend hours looking into his Prussian blue eyes, which have tiny white spikes shooting out from the pupil, while I brush my fingers over his temples, dark brows, straight nose, seriously tempting full lower lip, wicked mustache, and trimmed beard. I want to grab on to his thick dark hair as he moves that incredible hard, muscled body in mine. I want to feel his legs tangled with mine when we sleep. And I want to do it all until there's no breath left in my ancient body.

Nat pokes her head between the front seats and asks, "Still in your Ethan fog?"

I smile. "I don't think I'll ever get out of my Ethan fog."

"Good news for you that I don't think he's ever going to get out of his Theresa fog."

"If you don't mind me asking," Gio says, "is today the first time you've met? 'Cause it sure seemed like you knew each other."

Before I really think about who I'm asking, I say, "Are you two able to keep a secret?"

They looked at each other and bust out laughing.

Well, duh. Gio grew up with a Don for a father, and Nat had to go into hiding to keep herself safe.

Nat says, "Ah, yeah. We can keep a secret."

"I knew that. I don't know why I asked."

"Go ahead, spill."

"We met through The Letter Club. We've been writing to each other for months."

"Ha," Gio shouts. "Did you know he'd be at lunch today?"

"No. And he didn't know I'd be there. But he figured out who I was when Nat told him about Sofia's wedding. I'd written to him about my young friend who was pregnant and was getting married right away. He put two and two together."

"No surprises there," Nat says. "He's a smart guy and a good detective."

"Yeah. That all comes through in his letters. He has a quick mind."

"There's something about reading a person's soul before you meet them," Nat says knowingly.

We fall into a comfortable silence until I say, "Beautiful wedding. Sofia was radiant, and Matteo is besotted."

"Totally gone for her," Gio says. "Couldn't've picked anyone better if I'd tried."

"The food was outrageous," Nat says. "Even the cake was good, and that's not always the case. They look pretty but taste like cardboard."

I chuckle. "We were so drunk by dessert, I'm surprised you remember the cake."

Gio slaps his hand on Nat's thigh and squeezes. "My Ace always remembers dessert."

"Was that body shaming wrapped in sugar?" Nat snaps.

"Baby, are you serious? There isn't an inch of you I don't love, and I sure as fuck don't want you to change a thing about that body."

She grins at me, then turns to him and says, "Just checking."

Now, I crack up.

***

Ever the gentleman, Gio brings my luggage and my cannolis into the house. Then he and Nat walk with me to my neighbors to get Boo, who jumps up and down when he sees me, and kisses everyone. Gio carries Boo's stuff into the house, then I get hugs and kisses good-bye. I stand in my doorway watching them drive off before shutting the door.

After I put the cannolis in the fridge, I get my laptop and open the letter I started writing to Ethan. How odd to read this now knowing he's friends with Nat and has probably heard all about Sofia and Matteo. I'll do anything to ensure Ethan's safety, and if keeping up the ruse is important, then I'm all over that.

Ross,

While I'm waiting for my ride to my friend's wedding, I thought I'd bring you up to date.

Last weekend I played fashion consultant. If you're rolling your eyes right now, it's okay. I'm so happy for my friend, I'm a little gushy, so bear with me. My friend doesn't want a traditional wedding dress, so she bought a lovely ivory dress with delicate pink, blue, and yellow flowers (you know I love flowers) down part of the front and part of the back of the dress from a department store. It's off the shoulder with a scallop neckline and sleeves. I'm not doing it justice, but she looks magical in it.

To top off the outfit, she has a wide pearl and crystal (fake, but good fake) headband that looks like a crown, it's that pretty. Of course, she has fancy shoes with crystals at the toes, and really high heels, which she needs since she's tiny and her man is tall.

Got to go. My ride is here. I'll finish telling you everything when I get home.

I'm back home now. Boo was happy to see me. His standard "You've been away too long" greeting is to jump and down, then give me kisses until I'm coated with dog goo. Nothing wrong with being kissed all over.

The wedding: When we got to where we were going, we checked in at a lovely hotel. Even though the wedding was small and not entirely traditional, everyone got dressed up, which I enjoy. Pretty dress, hair done up, more makeup than usual, spikey heels – it's not something I'd want to do every day, but every once in a while, it's fun.

The church was small and historic, and the priest was so old I was worried he wouldn't be able to stay standing. But the ceremony went off without a hitch. The bride looked like an angel, and her husband couldn't take his eyes off her. They are very taken with each other.

Since we were a small party, we had the wedding dinner at a fabulous restaurant that served traditional Italian food, Honestly, I don't remember ever eating such a good meal in a restaurant. The wine flowed all night, and we drank too much, which made for loud and happy conversations. We all talked over each other, and by the time the wedding cake was wheeled out, pretty much everyone was stupid drunk. Except the father of the bride, who is not the type of person to lose control. While I didn't keep an eye on him all night, I don't think he had more than a couple of glasses of alcohol, and we were there for over four hours.

The next day, three of us had lunch with friends. I didn't think I'd be hungry after all that food the night before, but this restaurant has mainly bar food, but some interesting dishes. They have a Kung Pao Brussel sprout dish I had to try, which was fantastic. The foodie in me also had to taste the Mexican corn salad, and that didn't disappoint either. No hair of the dog for me. I stuck to tea and bubbly water.

I had a great time. One of those memorable days you know you'll never forget.

Our friends were excellent company, funny and engaging, but too soon we had to leave to go home.

I'm going to unpack, do laundry, and feed Boo.

Back to work tomorrow.

Flower

I want to call him and tell him about my day. I want to hear his voice to make sure he's all right. I want him to be here so I can cook him dinner. I want him to hold me while we sleep.

I can't have what I want, so I write another letter, knowing he's cut off from his world while trying to put horrible people behind bars.

Ross,

Ugh, what a day. Not work. That went smoothly. But the minute I got in my car to head home my phone went off. First, my sister – older by three years – called to inform me we're having Thanksgiving at our parents' house since they don't want to drive to my sister's home to celebrate. For the past two years we've been going to my sister's because the day after Thanksgiving is her youngest daughter's birthday. We make it a double event. I got the full-on bitching and moaning tirade about how intractable our mother is, and my sister was in rare form today. While I don't disagree with her, at this point in our lives, she shouldn't be surprised.

For as long as I have memory, my mother, whose career was a homemaker, was cleaning or organizing something. If she wasn't washing the dishes – she eschewed the dishwasher – or scrubbing the floor, she was cleaning the bathroom. The closets and cabinets got rotated and wiped down regularly. Our garage was cleaner than the interior of most people's homes, and our yard was meticulous. Weeds wouldn't dare grow there.

One hundred percent true story: Our mother is a small woman, as in barely five feet tall. One day my sister and I come home from school and we hear vague banging noises. We walk through the house and look out the back to see if for some reason our dad is home doing yardwork. When we don't see anything out of the ordinary, we go into the kitchen and our mother is standing inside the refrigerator – the freezer was on top and the model was old – cleaning it from top to bottom. All the shelves were on the counter – what we must've heard banging – along with the food, and she's inside muttering about how filthy everything is. She used strong cleaner, probably some bleach solution, and was coughing while she's inside that oblong box scrubbing like her life depended on it.

That is not an extreme story, but an emblematic one.

She, way more than our father, needs to control her environment, and she doesn't like to deviate from the known or the plan. She's been to my sister's for Thanksgiving the past two years and has been there in years previous. No way was going to my sister's house a surprise. But by our mother's standards, since my sister mentioned it ten days before Thanksgiving, my mother said that it was last minute and she couldn't be there with such short notice. The best part of the story is my sister lives fifteen miles away from our parents, while it's over an hour drive for me to get to either of them.

Apparently, my sister tried to get my mother to change her mind, but when she told my sister she could have Thanksgiving without her and Dad, that was the final straw. Hence, the phone call to me.

One of the consequences of being in my profession is my family thinks I can "shrink" wayward family members into good behavior or compliance. What everyone seems to forget is that those people are my family too, and we have dynamics of our own. Regardless, my sister was on a tear, and to keep her from breaking the full set of Waterford crystal glasses my parents bought as a fifth anniversary present – yes, my sister likes to threaten the Waterford regularly, and the glasses are really pretty so it would be a shame for her to smash them against the dining room wall – I agreed to call our mother.

At this juncture, I should've driven home, changed my clothes, spent some time with Boo, and had a glass of wine in my hand when I spoke to our mother. But, in the interests of getting what I knew would be a fruitless endeavor done as quickly as possible, I sat in my car, in the parking lot behind my office building, and made the call.

Two minutes into the conversation, I gave up. Mom was loaded for bear and waiting for me to ring. She picked up so fast, it was as if her finger was poised over the button. Immediately, she snarled, "I knew she would use you to get me to change my mind." All hope of détente was lost before I fired my opening salvo. I tried for a couple of minutes, said I'd see her on Thursday, and hung up. Then I went home, changed my clothes, and spent some time with Boo. I made sure I had a glass of wine in my hand before I called my sister to tell her the happy news.

Things devolved from there. I'd failed the challenge, and all hope was lost for a joyful Thanksgiving dinner. Did I mention my sister can be a little melodramatic? In less than an hour, which might be a new world record, I managed to talk her around, and promised I'd get there early to be part of the fortification team. The other member of the team is my sister's sister-in-law, Andie, who I adore. She's the antithesis of everything my mother treasures in a "young woman": dresses like a lady – don't get me started – has an "acceptable" profession – FYI, I don't – is married to a "good provider" – as if a woman can't provide for herself – and she has at least one child by the time she's thirty.

Andie is five-nine, is built like a Vegas headline stripper, has different color hair every time I see her, dresses in super-bright t-shirts she wears under farmer's overalls, and has a variety of vintage Doc Martens boots, mostly red. My favorite is the bright red pair with white polka dots.

Andie's thirty-nine, has never been married, has been living with a fairly well-known rock star for about thirteen years – who I pray is coming on Thursday – and Andie is a well-regarded sculptor. Andie's older brother is my brother-in-law, Sebastian, who is a tenured English professor, and used to be my sister's college professor – he's ten year older than her so it's not as scandalous as our mother makes it out to be – who "charmed" my sister into eloping when she was a junior, and they didn't start having kids until six years ago.

Families… You gotta love 'em.

The in-law parents moved to Taos, New Mexico after "Sebastian was finally married off," stating, "Our work here is done."

Ahhh, I see you're getting a clearer picture of what it will really mean when we all descend on my parents' home on Thanksgiving.

Don't worry. I know a few good attorneys.

Flower

Melrose, Massachusetts
Ethan
Deeper

After we leave the restaurant, we walk to the SUV where I ask Adam to drive so I don't give in to the near overwhelming desire to follow Theresa to Connecticut. He nods, and then drags his keys out of his front pocket. He doesn't say a word, but he knows watching her leave tore me up. The ride back to Melrose is quiet, and I need the silence to get my head back in the game.

As soon as Adam and I pull in the driveway, our next-door neighbor, Edwin, a retired comptroller, comes across his yard and says with urgency, "A very muscular, rather tall Hispanic man was at your front door a couple of hours ago. He knocked a few times and did something on his phone before he got in his car and drove away. I didn't have time to write down the license plate number, but I'd recognize him and the car if I see him again."

Well, shit. They should give Edwin an assignment. Instead of watching them, keep an eye on the Russians across the street. "Thanks, man, but that's our friend Ernesto. We crossed wires and missed each other."

Edwin looks disappointed there isn't some espionage involved. This is what happens when too many people watch *Jack Ryan* and *Bosch*. "Okay then. Have a good evening." Edwin walks off with slumped shoulders and heads into his house.

The "something on his phone" is the reason why we left Boston. Fernando, now known as Ernesto, has drive-by duty, and he knocked to communicate to Cam, now known as Simon, who is on duty in the house, that we were on our way back. I hate these fuckin' undercover names.

Intentionally, we're keeping communication low tech whenever possible. Fernando's text to Adam was in code, and we're using our phones sparingly. We tell all the newbies, watching *The Wire* is like required reading for coursework.

Once inside, we head upstairs where we've set up shop. The side window of the master bedroom gives us a clear shot of the Russians' house. Behind dark curtains with cutouts where surveillance cameras are embedded, no one could guess what we're doing or that we have a mini control center in this room.

Cam looks up from the monitors and gives us a chin lift.

"Anything?" Adam asks.

"Quiet day," Cam says. "The two who troll the clubs went out to get food, and came back about a half hour ago. Otherwise, nothing."

"Damn, I wish we had ears inside," I mutter.

"We need to catch one of those fuckers dropping a roofie in a girl's drink, and get him to roll. Then we'll get our wire."

"We pick up any of them, the whole house decamps and scatters," Adam says. "They don't care what happens to their 'colleagues.' It's all about making bank. And to do that, they need to dope and rope."

"Cold muthafuckas." Cam stands and stretches, then says, "I'm gonna eat, chill, and catch some Zs. I'll be back on at midnight."

"Right," I say. "I'll take next shift."

Adam and Cam leave and I stick in the earbud connected to the laptop, and fix my stare on the screen. It's going to be a long night.

***

I've always been a light sleeper. Even as a kid, I heard the dogs snoring, when someone got up in the middle of the night to use the bathroom, and when the early birds drove past our house on their way to work before sunrise. Flower on the brain was bad enough. Theresa on the brain is pure torture. I close my eyes and I feel her lips on mine, her legs wound around my body, her soft hair in my hands. I smell her light floral scent, taste her sweetness on my tongue, feel her juicy ass in the palm of my hands, and I can't sleep.

Shit. I can hardly breathe.

Over the years, I've learned if I don't get five hours a night, I'm no good to anybody, especially myself. I'm part of a team, and we need to stay sharp for each other. I've never been daredevil. I take calculated risks, and minimize my exposure to dangerous situations by being smart, alert, and prepared.

I try again. I close my eyes and see Theresa's small hand entwined with mine, and somehow that grounds me. We have the chance to build something solid and lasting. I'm not going to do anything to fuck that up. That means I have to stay strong and keep myself healthy. I take deep breaths and visualize a yard with trees and flower beds. A cool breeze is blowing and rustling the trees' leaves. I start to drift. It's peaceful here. This yard is a sanctuary that serves as a buffer from the harsh realities life shoves in our faces every day. My body relaxes, and I feel myself falling into a space between here and the pull of sleep.

The moment I'm there, ready to go under, I hear it. Someone's outside the house, and they're not being particularly quiet about it. Silently, I grab my gun, yank on my jeans, and pull my shirt off the back of the chair. I hear the intruder moving west, to the back of the house, and as I pass Adam's room, I pause and chamber my weapon, knowing that sound will wake him. As he slips out of bed, I touch my ear so he stops and listens. His gaze locks with mine when he hears the intruder, and he indicates he'll follow me.

I make my way down the hall and crouch behind the kitchen island waiting for the intruder to make his move. Adam joins me behind the island, and both of our heads turn when we hear Cam coming down the stairs. The moment he sees us, he crouches and frog walks to our position.

All the windows have blackout shades or curtains, including the small window in the back door. We changed out the locks and added deadbolts to all the doors. Cameras are placed strategically around the yard, under the eaves, and one over the back door and another over the front door are intentionally visible. The alarm system is rigged to the windows and doors, and any breach will be sent to the Melrose PD, as well as the FBI.

The doorknob jiggles, and the sound of someone trying to pick the lock in the knob makes me think this idiot is a garden variety break-and-grab asshole. I signal Cam to go back upstairs and call 9-1-1.

Adam and I wait while the mastermind fumbles for a minute or two before he gets the lock open only to realize there's a deadbolt in the door. Now he has two choices. Back off, or break the window and try to reach in to get to the interior locking mechanism. That'll be difficult – intentionally – since the thick blackout shade is sealed to the door.

The intruder walks off the back stoop, probably looking for a rock or something to smash the window. Definitely not a professional. Before he returns to the door, we hear two sets of footfall circling to the back. The cops are here, and we want the locals do their thing.

Two beats go by then a heavy thud hits the north side of the house.

They got him.

Adam and I stand and stick our weapons into the backs of our pants. As we wait for the cops' knock at our front door, Adam stretches out the bottom of his tee, then pulls it down. I button up my shirt. Cam comes to the top of the stairs and sees us leaning against the wall waiting. He nods and returns to the surveillance room.

A couple of minutes later, there's the knock at the front door.

We wait a few moments, creep up the stairs, make noise coming down, and then we turn on the lights.

Adam asks, "Who's there?"

"Officer Batson, Melrose PD," a deep voice responds.

Adam moves the curtain alongside the window next to the door to "check" that it is indeed Officer Batson, then turns the locks and opens the door.

Batson says, "You guys all right?"

"A little rattled, but fine, officer. Thanks. Do you want to come in?" Batson turns and nods to an officer in a second cruiser, who takes off, presumably to book the wannabe intruder. The cruiser's lights are going, strobing red and blue, cutting through the night.

Batson comes in, and we all walk to the kitchen, where a lone store-bought pumpkin pie sits on the island. Adam, Cam, and I took turns eating turkey sandwiches and chips in front of the TV, watching football. It's the first Thanksgiving I wasn't home with my family.

"What happened?" Adams asks.

"We apprehended a male, mid-to late twenties, prowling around your back door." Batson looks to the door. "Did he break the glass?" Batson walks across the kitchen and looks at the floor.

"No, but we think we heard the knob jiggle."

Batson lifts his chin, then says, "I'll be back after I try to lift prints off the backdoor and knob."

"We'll turn on the outside lights for you," Adam says.

"'Preciate it." Batson leaves out the front, and on his way says, "Lock up."

After he leaves Adam and I grin at each other. "He's tight," Adam says.

"Yeah, but he's dying to know if we are who we seem." I turn on the outside lights, and we both return to our rooms to divest ourselves of our guns.

About ten minutes later, Batson knocks again, and Adam answers.

"Don't know if I got anything, but we have the intruder." He sticks his hand inside his top pocket and pulls out a couple of business cards. "Call me if you find anything, or if you need anything. I'll be in touch within the next couple of days."

Adam sticks out his hand. "Thank you, officer."

Batson shakes it, turns on his heel, and leaves. We lock up and turn off the inside and outside lights. Then we head upstairs to look at the surveillance footage from the exterior cameras.

What we find does not make us happy. Our "novice" is no novice. He played us, tried to draw us out – why he wasn't so quiet – to find out who moved into the house across the street from his base of operation. The man Natalia ID'd as Viktor apparently doesn't mind pleading guilty to trespassing, a misdemeanor. I'd bet my boots Viktor wore gloves and the only thing the cops can charge him with is trespassing. They sure don't have enough for attempted breaking and entering.

First shot across the bow, and we're in great shape. We called the cops, the fucktards across the street saw Adam open the door and let the cop in. All they know is they can't see in the house, and we have a deadbolt on the back door. Big deal. A lot of people like privacy, and most people have deadbolts on their doors. Especially if they live in a major metropolitan area.

This attempt to learn if we're who we're pretending to be told us all kinds of things. Not the least of which is those bastards don't want to have to move their operation again. My guess, other arms of their organization have girls already, and they plan to hold them in the house across the street.

After waking Skip, he says we're having a remote meeting tomorrow with him and Rashad. No way those POS across the street are acting alone. There's a network, and we need to pull in other JTTFs to find out who else from the Lebedevsky *Bratva* is on the ground in the Northeast, and how coordinated their effort is.

***

Seven days later, we're having another remote meeting with Skip and Rashad. Fernando's up in rotation and is staying in the house with me and Adam. Everyone knows the nearly nonexistent activity across the street is a ruse, and while waiting for the shit to hit the fan we've been accessing reports and information gathered by various law enforcement agencies. The fact that we've found nothing doesn't mean there's nothing to find, but that if there are groups affiliated with *Bratva*, they're not hitting the radar, which is not surprising. Had Jonas not suspected something was amiss, and his father wasn't with the FBI, the chances of us knowing these guys exist are low. Even after the girls were roofied, the likelihood we would've ascribed the incident to a human trafficking ring is again, unfortunately, low.

Rashad had agreed with me, Cam, and Adam, and took our suggestion to pull in other area JTTFs to the SAC – Special Agent in Charge George Randall. If the wheels of justice grind slowly, decision-making at the FBI moves at a half-speed snail's pace. But today – which is a lot faster than I expected – we're hearing Randall got the higher-ups to agree the scope of our investigation has to widen.

Later, at three, we're conferencing with all the JTTFs in the Northeast. I'm particularly interested in hearing what the New Haven and Albany offices have to say since they're along what we've dubbed the college corridor.

Right now, though, I'm in my room shifting through the mail I picked up at the Saugus post office box this morning. All the bills to this house come in Drew's name, and all my personal bills are being forwarded to a P.O. box near the office, which one of the admins visits weekly. I left my checkbook with signed blank checks for the admin to pay the bills, and since my paycheck is direct deposit, everything's covered. The mail that comes to the box in Saugus – near a few shopping centers so I get a few things done in one go – is from my family, and Theresa's included in that group.

There are five letters. One from Trask, my brother, two from my mom, and two from Theresa. I save Flower's for last.

My brother has a buddy from college who lives in Cannon, a coastal community on the Oregon shore, and he keeps a boat a few miles south at Wheeler Marina. I've been out with them a few times. Sweet Monterey 224FS. Trask goes about once every couple of months to clear his head. He leaves his house early on Saturday morning and gets back home by Sunday evening. His letter is all about his boating weekend with Greg, which he usually takes before Thanksgiving for fortification.

My mom, who talks a blue streak, writes about the same. Over the two letters, I get caught up on all the Fiddler's Rest gossip, including what's doing at Gusk's Hardware. She spent a page on detailed updates about her greenhouse, and another on my dad's latest woodshop project, which is a new coat tree for the front foyer. Mom's decided the old one is too beat up and doesn't work with her "new aesthetic." I don't even want to know what the hell that is, but when I write back, I'll ask because she wants me to. That's why she dropped the phrase.

I open Theresa's first letter, and it's her way of letting me know she's home safe and misses me. The flirting is subtle, and makes my dick ache more than it does every time I think of her. I'm hard just knowing she's touched the paper. Reading about spikey heels, and her saying, "Nothing wrong with being kissed all over" is torture. From this driveway to hers is seventy-five miles. I could be there in less than two hours. The only thing that keeps from going is knowing I'd be putting her in danger. I'd never do that. Not ever.

Her next letter is filled with family drama. I swear, if I close my eyes, I can hear her telling me about this shit while we're sitting having dinner in the kitchen, recapping our day. Something I never thought about having, and now I miss. Sure, my folks did it, and I had that when I was a kid, but for myself, never.

I want that. I want to know all the craziness that makes her family tick because I want her to be my family. Yeah, I know, it's fucking insane to be this attached to someone I met once. But I've known her for months, and she'd already gotten under my skin deep. Indelible. Like a tattoo only I can see. Meeting her in person sealed the deal. Kissing her, tasting her – without a doubt, she's my forever. But for real, she was mine before she walked into that restaurant.

I reread her letters a couple more times to commit them to memory, then I take all the letters into the kitchen, set them on fire, and let them burn out in the sink. When there's nothing but ash, I wash it down the drain, then pour in bleach to make sure everything is gone and is irretrievable.

As I stare at the drain, for the first time since I became a cop, I think this is a fucked-up way to live. Don't get me wrong, I love my job, and I believe in what I'm doing. But no way am I bringing this to my doorstep every night. I want my wife and kids to sleep soundly, without worrying about where I am and how many more weeks before I'm able to come home. I don't want to burn Flower's letters. I want to treasure them. Without those letters, I would've never found the person to fill the emptiness inside me I didn't even know I had.

***

Three o'clock meeting. Having a screen split seven ways is giving me a headache, and we haven't even started. George Randall is sitting with Rashad and Skip in what looks like our conference room. I don't know any of the other offices' team members, except one of the agents from New Haven who's been up to the Boston office a couple of times tying up a couple of old cases. His transfer made my job possible. One of the agents from the New York office had been out to Portland a few years back, but we had one meeting together, and no contact since.

Everyone's read our brief. No need to rehash what they already know. George begins by asking if the other teams have anything to share. Not surprisingly, the New York office has plenty to say about the *Bratva* since Brighton Beach is and has been home to the Russian mob in the US for decades. Ultimately, though, they know of *Vory* (made men) who run huge prostitution rings, but no one has heard of a dope-and-rope operation used for human trafficking, especially not on college campuses.

One of the NYPD on the JTTF says the PD gets hundreds of doping reports coming out of clubs and bars, but none of it seems coordinated. He told us he'd have the reports pulled and analyzed, but my guess, they won't find a pattern.

The NY agent I met reminded us that usually the human trafficking went the other way. Predominantly Ukrainian and Russian women trafficked out of that region to the Middle East, Europe, and the US.

All of the members of the NY office talked about how the Lebedevskys are known players on the field, but they don't have a huge presence in New York, and their specialty is limited to running guns. The Newark office is also aware of a Lebedevsky presence, but again it's small, and it's limited to guns.

We agree to keep each other updated, and now that they have all the photos and IDs we have, they'll check their sources. But making this wide net play is the long game, and since it "seems" these dope-and-ropes are happening only on our patch, we're the lead, and we're on our own.

Fuck.

***

The other JTFFs signed off and we stayed on screen with George, Rashad, and Skip, who'd called Benita, Cam, Luke, and Niles in for a team strategizing session that lasted an hour. Now, after a shitty day, I want to talk to Flower. Actually, I want to get in my car and drive home – to our home – then walk in the front door and have Boo jump on me to get his body rub, and to hear Theresa say, "Come get a beer and tell me about your day."

As fantasies go, it's not sexy and elaborate, but it's what I wish for day in and day out for the next sixty years.

Hey babe –

If your family decides to do a reality TV gig, you'll be rolling in bank within a week. People would eat that shit up, especially with a rock star in the fam. Would I know their music? I'm looking forward to reading about Thanksgiving at your folks' house.

Heard from my family. They're well. My mom's hard at work in the greenhouse. She's

either harvesting or planting. She grows a lot of veggies: carrots, green beans, snap peas, potatoes, beets, and cabbage. That's all I remember, but I know there's lots more. Have to say, carrot cake made with homegrown carrots tastes great.

Dad's busy in his workshop. A hobby turned sideline. He makes wooden furniture, and over the years, neighbors have "commissioned" him for benches, porch swings, kitchen tables, and he made a desk for one guy's office. Massive thing. Took *professional movers to get it in place. Dad refuses to accept money, but will barter, and enjoys the hell out of it. For instance, the massive desk was for a guy who owns an insurance agency. Dad always thought the guy jacked up the rates, and had never used him until the desk. Dad said he got the better deal. He negotiated a premium umbrella policy for the house and cars, and told Mom they were saving about $600 a year by switching policies. Mom figures that desk would've cost the guy about $10k, so they're going to have less expensive and better insurance for the next twenty years.*

What'd you make for dinner tonight? Are you baking anything for Thanksgiving?

Does Boo play Frisbee? Give him a few extra rubs from me.

Enjoy your Thanksgiving, babe.

Ross

Dutchford to rural CT outside Manchester, then Avon, CT
Theresa
Brouhaha

Ross,
So much to say, I figured I'd document the next few days and send it all at once so we don't cross-post.

<u>Tuesday</u>
As if my sister and mother weren't enough of the family dose, my cousin called. Not Ziggy. This call was from Max, the one who always takes care of Ziggy. Actually, taking care of everyone else except herself is usually Max's problem. She's full of tough love for any soul in need, and she's the BEST friend anyone could ever have, but she doesn't see to herself. I don't mean in the grooming, clothing, socializing way. She's beautiful and well put together all the time. For all outward appearances, Max has the world on a string. The only two people who know the truth about what roils around inside of her are her childhood friend, Lola, and me.

Lola is pregnant. Yes, another one. I told you there's something in the water. Lola is not having an easy pregnancy, which means Max isn't sitting in Lola's kitchen drinking homemade lemonade – Lola makes the best lemonade – bitching and moaning about whatever in general or anything in specific because Max doesn't want to stress out Lola.

The call from Max was all about her skating on emotional thin ice, which is not somewhere she ventures. Loooong story short, she harbors MAJOR guilt about something that happened over ten years ago in college to someone else for which she holds herself responsible, but she wasn't. Not even close.

A confession: I chose my specialty because of Max. She's two years younger than I am, and this thing happened when I was a senior in college. She went to a college not too far from mine, and I was the one who held her hand after the incident. When I knew that my being there for her wasn't enough, I was the one who convinced

Max to go to therapy. When I saw what a difference it made, I decided that work was for me.

Ninety percent of the time, Max breezes through life, making sure she doesn't go near that guilt well. Every now and again, she has a "moment," and we talk it through, typically over a few phone calls. Then she moves on. What she has never done since "the incident" is make herself emotionally vulnerable. If she gets a whiff she might be more than casually interested in somebody, she backs off and moves on. But a new man somehow ambushed her and crawled right into her heart when she wasn't looking, and now she's nearing meltdown.

I've begged her to tell the guy what's going on. He's way into her, and from the little she's said, he sounds like the type of man who will treat her and the information gently and with care. She refuses. Of all the traits Max has that makes her strong, stubbornness is at the top of the list. This time though, it's doing her in and I can't seem to be able to get through, which has never happened. That tells me she's scared out of her mind, which means she's fallen for this guy, and she's drowning in it.

Honestly, my sister and mother's drama are much easier to handle.

Wednesday

I called Max and left a message. If I don't hear from her by tomorrow, I'm running her to ground. She knows this about me, so I'm thinking I'll hear from her.

Boo doesn't play Frisbee, but that's my fault because I don't play Frisbee. We play ball in the park, and he has a basket full of durable toys to chew on and play with in the house. I've noticed he jumps in the air to catch a ball, so maybe he'll take to Frisbee. I'll go on YouTube and watch some Frisbee vids. I've heard it's all about wrist action, but I'm not what you'd call an athlete. I'll let you know how that goes.

Tonight, I had a salad for dinner in preparation for tomorrow when I'll eat as if it's my last meal. Also, I'm baking a German chocolate cake as my niece's birthday cake, and I'm baking an apple pie, a cherry pie, and a yam/pumpkin pie with a crispy cinnamon crust.

Ten minutes before I was headed to bed, my sister called and begged me to stop at her place so we could ride over to our parents' house together, as if she didn't have two kids and a husband as a buffer.

<u>Thursday</u>

My mother called to make sure I baked the cake and the pies. Max called to tell me Happy Thanksgiving, and she's fine so stop hovering. I didn't hear from my sister and figured that was a good thing.

Normally, I'd leave Boo home, but given how long I'm going to be gone, I can't do it. He's been to my sister's house before and he loves her dog, Eloise, who's a mutt rescue that looks like a small brown border collie. My sister, who has acreage, fenced in about ½ acre of her property for Eloise. Boo will be in heaven – outdoors all day, and room to run with a friend.

I have to leave earlier than expected to get to my sister's, talk her off a ledge, and get Boo settled before we head over to what will surely be an entertaining Thanksgiving. I'll catch you up when I get home.

Home. Sebastian gets the outstanding husband, and a great father of the year award. When I walked into a house I'd been sure would be filled with pandemonium, instead I found my nieces, Valeria and Austen, sitting in the family room on the floor, both in hot pink leggings and little black booties. Valeria was in a multicolored striped long-sleeved A-line dress, and Austen in the same type of dress but in purple. It's her third birthday so right now the only colors in her life are pink and purple. Both girls' hair was in ponytails, and white ribbons were tied in bows around the bands holding up the ponytails. Eloise was lying between them, and they were all watching Moana.

Figuring I'd meet a different tableau, I'd taken Boo out back and put him in Eloise's yard before coming in the house.

The girls looked up, saw me, got up, came over and gave me hugs and kisses, then went back to the family room where Valeria rewound the video back to where it'd been before I interrupted them.

Sebastian was in the kitchen watching us as he was putting foil wrap over my sister's scalloped potatoes. The long Pyrex dish with her baked macaroni was already covered.

When I asked Sebastian, who everyone calls Baz, what was up, he smiled and told me he'd taken the girls and for an early breakfast at IHOP, then they went to the park where they ran off the sugar high, and he made sure they walked long enough for them to reach the little girl version of relaxed. While they were gone, my sister had time and peace to make her two dishes. When Baz and the girls got home, my sister went in to take a shower and the girls had quick baths and got dressed. Baz did their hair.

As he was wrapping up his rundown, my sister came into the kitchen looking the picture of serenity in a winter white cable-knit sweater that rested on her hips, worn over a pair of ruby red wide wale cords under which were black cowboy boots. I gave her a big hug and she said in my ear, "He got a blowjob last night before he got laid, and he got a blowjob this morning. I didn't have to ask him to do a damn thing."

Incentivizing through reward clearly works well for Baz.

Since all was well in their world, there was no need to talk my sister off a ledge.

Baz loaded up their Range Rover, including transferring my dishes to their vehicle, while I took Eloise out to Boo. They were enthralled with each other to the point where Boo didn't even notice me walking away.

We pulled into my parents' driveway – long uphill driveway – at the same time Andie and Lars were getting out of his – I have to stop here and let you know, anyone who doesn't drool over this vehicle has something wrong with them – new Mansory Lamborghini Urus Venatus. It had the shiniest black paint I've ever seen on a vehicle. It's a crossover SUV, but it's nothing like my RAV4, and it sure as hell isn't a hybrid. Lars said it had shit gas mileage, maybe 20 mph on the highway, if he's lucky. But it's a beauty. Along the grill work, which is like a futuristic Mad Max kind of grill, there's red piping that also goes around the wheels, and there's one red line down the side of the vehicle, about the height of the door handles. There's piping around the tail pipes, and one red line bisecting each side-view mirror. Oh, and piping over the small spoiler in the back and along the bottom of the carriage. It's wicked to look at, and damn it goes fast. Lars took me, Laura, my sister, and Baz out for a quick spin, and holy hell, what fun. It has red and black interior and it's totally high tech.

When we got back all hell broke loose. Andie had taken the girls, who weren't interested in going for a ride, into the house, and told my parents where the rest of us were. My mother was waiting by the front door and went into a tirade about how rude we were for not coming into the house straight away.

Honestly, Lars is a prince 'cause he doesn't need that shit, and he could've said a lot of choice words to my mother. But he gave her a peace sign, told us he'd see us inside, and he sauntered in the house like he owned it.

Baz waited until Lars was gone before letting my mother have it, and I swear, I wanted to applaud. He told her we were having Thanksgiving at her house instead of his and his wife's because she can't get the stick out of her ass long enough to realize how lucky she is to have two fantastic daughters and two amazing granddaughters, and if she didn't cut this shit out, she'd be seeing a lot less of all of us. Then he stomped into the house, leaving me and Laura with our mother, who looked pale but tried to save face and said, "I never," and then walked into the house.

Laura turned to me and said, "He earned the blowjobs when he took on the girls this morning. But what he just said to Mom...he's getting a blowjob every morning for the next two weeks."

Valeria and Austen love their nana and poppi, and we didn't want to do anything to upset that apple cart. I sat next to my dad and across from Baz, who had Austen between him and Laura. Valeria sat next to Laura. Lars, then Andie were to my right. Andie nonplusses my mother, which meant Valeria had all her nana's attention. The food was good. My mother's housekeeper had prepared the dishes yesterday. All my mother had to do was warm everything, and, of course, she made a fuss like she'd been cooking for weeks. My sister's baked macaroni is one of my all-time favorites, so I scarfed, hoping for a carb coma. Actually, the conversation at dinner wasn't too stilted since everyone focused away from Mom. We sang "Happy Birthday" to Austen, ate dessert, and left.

The real fun started at Baz and Laura's, where we all relaxed, talked, drank, and laughed. Andie keeps photos of her sculptures on her phone, and she let me see the work that'll be in her new show at J-Gestia Gallery in Soho in NYC. She insisted we all come to the opening, and I'm going to go. Baz and Laura go to all Andie's openings, even some in Italy when they can swing it.

I drank too much to drive home, and spent the night. Boo was happy to sleep in bed with me – Laura is cool about that stuff – and we left after breakfast. Baz made "birthday" pancakes and we sang "Happy Birthday" again, and then Austen opened her presents. I got her Design and Drill Creative Workshop. It's a STEM drill and construction toy.

No office hours the day after Thanksgiving, and I don't go shopping on Black Friday. I'm not into crowds and frenzy buying. Today's a home spa day. Face masks, lots of lotions for different parts of my body, and copious napping.

Happy Thanksgiving.

Flower

What I couldn't tell Ethan – not because I don't want him to know, but I worry about putting him in an awkward position at work – is that more happened at Thanksgiving than I shared in the letter.

To backtrack, right after we cut Austen's cake, my phone pinged and I had a message to call my service immediately. My patients know if they call my service off-hours, on the weekend, or during holidays, I'll return the call. I stayed to sing "Happy Birthday," then asked my dad if I could use his study to make a work-related call. When he said, "Sure," I went down the hall and around the corner to his home office, and then closed the door before I sat in the big chair behind his desk and called my service.

The holidays are stressful for everyone for different reasons. For one seventeen-year-old boy they are particularly horrendous because his father died of cancer last month, and his mother has never worked outside the home.

Ramon, my patient, is seeing me on what I tell families is my scholarship fund. I don't have a scholarship fund, though I wish I did. I use the moniker so the families don't feel beholden because I'm really giving free visits to my patients. I get these "scholarship fund" kids when a guidance counselor or school psychologist has a severe case and wants to get the kid into therapy.

I started to see Ramon when his father was in hospice care at their home, and over the past few months it's become clear the weight of the entire family – he has three younger sisters – has fallen on this poor kid's shoulders.

I talked to Ramon for about forty minutes, and he breaks my heart. He's such a good guy who's looking for a miracle, and he doesn't know what to do to keep everyone and everything afloat. On Monday, I'm going to speak to my friends at the garden center and ask them to give Ramon a part-time job to work after school and on the weekends. The money won't be enough to pay a mortgage, but it'll make him feel useful and like he's contributing while I get a social worker friend of mine from Social Services to go over to the home to help the family.

While I was on the phone with Ramon, absently, I was staring at paperwork on my father's desk. Something caught my eye, and after the call ended, I picked up a copy of a letter from my father to a business associate overseas. Since most of the business my father does as the executive manager for an import company is with purveyors of fine foods from the Mediterranean, the letter in and of itself was no big deal. But I'd never seen the company letterhead before. Or, if I had, it didn't trip anything until today.

Substantial Food Imports
An ADC Holding company

When I was fighting with Don Di Caro about paying my medical bills, I knew some of how much he was shelling out because, by accident, one of my therapist's agency had mailed the Don's receipt to me. The name and address of his company was on the receipt: ADC Holding.

While everyone was helping clear the table, I pulled my father aside and asked him if Don Di Caro had always owned Substantial Food Imports. My father's answer was, "Leave it, *cara*."

A yes or no would make me curious, but "leave it" means he's hiding something and there's a story he doesn't want me to know.

On the drive home, my mind started reeling. Did Don Di Caro send Sofia to see me nearly two years ago because my father works for him? Did he provide all that care and pay for all those bills out of a sense of obligation beyond what he'd explained to me every time we went 'round and 'round about him footing the bill?

I know my father. I'd sooner get my mother to dye her hair pink than have my father spill the beans. I could ask Don Di Caro, but he'd stonewall or deflect. He's never lied to me, but there've been plenty of times I didn't get a straight answer out of him.

Maybe I'll talk to Max about it. Over the years we've hypothesized about the brothers' split, but we've never come up with anything solid. I'll call her over the weekend to check on her, but use this as my entrée to see how she's doing.

Melrose, MA
Ethan
North

The FBI's Boston office covers Massachusetts and the states due north. Although there are ten satellite offices in the four-state area, the Boston headquarters runs the show. As I lie awake replaying the three o'clock conference call in my head, it's bothering the fuck out of me that not one other JTTF has a lead or anything we can tie to our operation. Then I think about Maine, New Hampshire, and Rhode Island and decide we need to get those satellite offices involved in this investigation. I figure George Randall has thought the same thing, but since he didn't say anything during our one-hour team strategizing session, I'll reach out to Skip to set up another call to run this by him.

Luke's supposed to rotate in on Saturday. After he gets settled, I'll go over to Saugus, do some shopping, and pick up my mail.

I'm in bed staring at the ceiling, wondering if Theresa sleeps soundly or if the shooting invades her dreams. I hope it's the former, but if it's not, that I can't be there to hold her to make her feel safe is fucking with me. I need to lend her my strength to absorb whatever residual effects she's suffering due to yet another POS who thought it was okay to shoot his ex.

These thoughts are not helping. I close my eyes and it takes a while, but I'm able to find that peaceful place I've been in before: the backyard with the trees and flower beds. I picture myself lying on a lounger in the middle of that green space and finally, I begin to drift. As I do, I swear I can smell Theresa's skin.

***

Skip is receptive to getting the satellite offices involved, and we expect to hear back from him and Rashad by this afternoon. I'm putting the breakfast mess in the dishwasher when there's a knock on the front door.

Fernando is at the top of the stairs, and Adam comes out of his bedroom, but doesn't move down the hall. Both of them have their weapons drawn. I move to the door, but stand to the side, my back against the wall when I shout, "Yeah. What's up?"

"It's Ed from next door."

I see Fernando move off, and I hear Adam walk away. Then I open the door and step outside. "Hey, Ed. Something you need?" I walk down the steps to about halfway down the walkway, forcing Ed to move away from the house to talk to me. Which he does.

"Actually, it's something you and Drew might need." Ed's looking up at me, and his expression says *I know something you don't know.*

"And that is?"

His voice drops and he dips his head. "The house across the street. Three doors down...don't look, but they've been watching your house."

Jesus fuck. We know that, but how does Ed? "Why would you think that?"

Ed glances up at me but keeps his voice low. "A few days ago, I was out front trimming the rhododendron when this flash hits my eyes. I look up and don't see anything, and, frankly, I wrote it off to a passing car's reflection." He stops, and I nod for him to continue. Clearly the dude is all worked up to get to *the good part.* "Yesterday, when I was weeding around the weeping cherry trees, the same thing happened. I didn't look up until a few minutes later, then it happened again, and I saw the flash coming from...that house." He's talking faster now. "This morning, after the missus went to get her hair done, I went up to the attic and brought my binoculars with me. Good ones. I belong to a bird-watching club." I give him my *I'm impressed* face to keep him going. "I went to the front of the house, and using my binoculars, I was able to see across the street through the slats in the vent. Sure enough, after a few minutes, I see the flash again. But this time, I can see a bit of a tube, like a telescope, parting the curtains in one of the upstairs rooms." He looks at me with wide eyes. "What do you make of that?"

Uh...that those assholes don't seem to be good at anything they do, which makes it that much more frustrating that we can't shut them down. "Perhaps they're bird-watchers like yourself."

He scrunches up his jowly face and says, "I hadn't thought of that, but it seems unlikely."

I've gotta get him to move off this. "Don't know much about bird-watching, but there sure are a lot of birds around here."

"True," he says, but seems reluctant to agree. "But *real* bird-watchers place themselves in the birds' natural habitat so we can see them in their environment. Almost all of the birds around here come for nest-making material and food."

"But some make their nests here. We removed a couple from under the eaves last weekend." We hadn't, but my father used to pull down one or two every autumn when he cleaned the gutters, so I knew it was plausible. "Maybe the folks across the street are watching the locals. You know, birds that made their homes here." I shrug. "Or maybe they're amateurs, and they're just starting out."

Ed sighs a couple of times. "You might be right."

"I'm sure it's innocuous. They might be stargazers and that's where they leave the telescope during the day." I dip my head to make Ed feel like we're in on this together. "Could be lots of things, but I'm thinking, in this neighborhood, it's innocent."

Ed's expression changes to resolute. "I certainly hope so. We've lived here for twenty-six

years, and the worst thing that's happened since we moved in was about ten years back when the McGillicuddy twins toilet-papered everyone's trees and cars on gate night."

I would've paid good money to see Ed's face that morning when he was leaving his house to go to work and came out to that mess. Trask and I used to do that shit. Total fun.

"I'm glad to hear it's as safe here as Drew and I had hoped." I point to the house. "Gotta get back to it, Ed, but thank you for looking out for us. We appreciate having such a good neighbor." Cop 101: When community policing, make the people you're talking to feel empowered by their actions to keep their neighborhood safe even if it's misguided. Remember, it's the officer's job to steer civilians to the right path when watching out for each other.

Yep. That puffed him up. "You're welcome, Nick. Happy to help." Off he goes, and I hope to hell he stays out of the attic with those fucking binoculars.

When I get back inside and share the conversation, Fernando says, "I don't think they're being sloppy because they're fuck-ups. Well, they're fuck-ups for sure, but not about that."

"Explain," Adam says.

"I'm thinking the obvious surveillance is like the obvious break-in attempt. They don't like not knowing who we are and what we're doing here, especially having moved in three weeks after they did."

"Shit." Adam shakes his head. "They're baiting us."

"Exactly," Fernando says. "It's a double-edged sword. We do and say nothing, they're more curious. We approach them, and that gives them what they want because then they know we're watching them too. We call the cops, we can't tell them we know our intruder was a frequent visitor to that house. And you know they're not going to send someone out to bother neighbors who have a telescope out the window. All our windows are covered and there's no underage children here, which would be one of the few reasons they'd talk to anyone who seems to be watching the neighborhood."

"Fuck," I mutter. "Best to play dumb and see what they do."

"One thing we need to do is up the blocking on this house," Adam says. "If they've tried to listen in – and they're close enough to use a pretty low-tech device – and found they can't get through, that's the biggest tell we have. Now that I think about it, they probably have been trying to listen in, and when they couldn't they reverted to visual surveillance."

"You gonna call it in?" I ask Fernando.

"Yeah," he grunts.

Two hours later, we're conferencing with Skip, who tells us Rashad had sent out a communique to the satellite offices and they got a hit. We sit waiting for the Portland, Maine office to come online. A woman appears on the screen and IDs herself as Special Agent Thea Grandeau.

After the introductions, she says, "I read your brief and it tracks with a case we're looking into in Portland. On Tuesday, October thirty-first, Halloween, three female students from Bowdoin College, about a half hour up the coast from Portland, were at a popular club in Portland that was hosting a Halloween party. Lots of costumes, which made the two guys who approached these girls stand out because they weren't in costumes. The girls said the two suspects talked with heavy accents, but they couldn't say from where.

"One of girls went off to dance with another guy, not associated with the two in question, and of the two girls who were left with the suspects, one reported seeing the taller of the two putting something in her drink. She told her friend she needed to go to the bathroom, and asked the friend to join her. Once they were in the bathroom, the girl told her friend what happened and they call nine-one-one. They waited in the bathroom until a female plainclothes officer came and got them. They found their other friend, and the three girls went with the officer and her partner to the police station to file a report. They gave reasonably detailed descriptions of the two suspects, and were then taken to their car. They returned to Bowdoin without incident.

"After reading your brief, we put out an inquiry to area PDs, as did the Bangor office. Portland PD supplied the report filed by the girls. I've forwarded that report to your ASAC. Based on the descriptions given, we believe our suspects are two of three individuals involved in your doping incident."

"You planning to talk to the girls?" I ask.

"I've reached out to them, and hope to see them on Monday at O-ten hundred."

Perfect. "Mind if I tag along?"

"Not at all."

We give our thanks and say our good-byes but stay on screen with Skip.

"It's about a two-hour drive to Portland," Skip tells me. "I suggest you leave by six or you'll be sitting in traffic half the way up."

"Will do, and I'll touch base when I get back Monday late afternoon."

Skip nods then clicks off.

"Fuckin' finally," Fernando says. "I knew they weren't concentrating in one place. Let's see if anything comes back from any of the other satellite offices."

"I'm betting more than one local LEO has a similar story," Adam says.

More shoptalk, then I'm reminded I'm on KP duty today, and head to the kitchen to make dinner.

***

Fernando leaves early the next morning, and Luke shows up after breakfast. He gets settled in the upstairs bedroom, and I head out to Saugus. I'm not even out of our neighborhood when I pick up the tail. Is this another case of being obvious, or are they that incompetent? I'm going for door number two, but regardless, I carry on as if the guy in the black Camry isn't on my ass. I head up Main Street and turn onto Lynn Fells Parkway and head to US 1 to Trader Joe's. Luke's a vegetarian and has a list a mile long of must-haves. There's a PetSmart next to Trader Joe's and I think of Boo. How I'm missing a dog I never met makes no sense, but he belongs to Flower, and she belongs to me. I buy six quarts of the cherry chocolate chip soy ice cream 'cause that stuff sounds good.

On the way out, I clock my tail, who parked one row behind me. Idiot.

Next up is Stop and Shop, where I load up on staples. They don't carry Adam's shampoo – he's like a girl about his hair – so I head down US 1 and go to Walgreens. The whole time, that asshole is right with me. Last stop is the post office, and as I always do, I take two large manila envelopes addressed to New England Patriots and make sure they're visible as I carry them into the building. Inside are requests to be put on the wait list for season tickets. I'm not interested in buying season tickets, but it's a good ruse. It takes me to the counter where I push across the big envelopes and my letters, which I keep in my inside jacket pocket. I ask the guy to get the mail out of my box, this way no one sees me going to the box. I take the four letters he passes to me, fold them, and then stuff them in my jacket pocket.

My tail follows me home, and Adam comes out and makes a show of helping me bring in the bags. I tell him and Luke about the tail, and they agree, it's more of the obvious shit to see how we react. The asshole must be disappointed since I acted like I didn't know he was there.

After everything's put away, I head to my room and see two letters from my mother, one from Trask, and a thick one from Theresa.

Trask catches me up on his family, and is all about missing me at Thanksgiving, and how it'll suck not to be with me on Christmas.

More of the same from my mother, along with detailed interior decorating changes that are in line with her new design aesthetic.

Flower's missive is the longest letter I've ever received in my life, and I go slow, reading every word like they hold the secret to life. And, in a way, they do. They're her gift to me when I can't be where I should be, with her. They're a part of her I get to savor in the absence of holding her in my arms while we watch a movie lying on the couch.

I'm not even on the second sentence and the words on the page turn into her voice in my head. God, I love her voice. Sexy, sultry, and throaty. Now I'm hard as tungsten steel, and I have to deep breathe for a couple of minutes to get my shit together.

No lie, this sucks in a way I've never experienced. It's a sunny Saturday, and everyone is out shopping for the holidays. Christmas trees and giant menorahs with screw-in bulbs instead of candles glow from almost every house in the neighborhood. To make sure we look like we belong here, I bought a door wreath today from Trader Joe's, and last weekend I strung those tiny white lights around the front door.

I hate that I'm not hanging lights on Theresa's and my home. That we don't have a tree lit up in our front window. That I'm not listening to her tell me about what she bought for which family member and why. That I'm not eating what I know is one of her fuckin' spectacular cupcakes right now.

If I don't calm down, I'm going to do something stupid. I close my eyes, picture her beautiful face, and start the letter over again.

Jesus, the woman is trying to kill me talking about blowjobs. I refuse to conjure that image in my head for fear I'll get in the car and drive straight to her house.

I keep reading, and decide one day I'll get her to tell me the long story about her cousin Max, who Flower clearly adores.

Thanksgiving sounds whacked. I'm not a fan of her mother's. I'm with Baz. She needs to take a look at what she's got and get her head out of her ass. The sister and husband sound cool, and now I know who the rock star is. He's not fairly well-known, he's an international superstar who drives an SUV that costs a quarter mil. He and Andie are definitely cool. I've seen pictures of her when a story about Lars was in the news. Flower was right. Andie does have the body of a Vegas headline stripper. The woman's a knockout.

I didn't miss the invite to meet Flower in NYC. I wouldn't go to the show, although I'm sure I'd enjoy it, but under no circumstances is anyone going to see me with her and her family. Too dangerous right now. I can't fucking wait until that's not the case.

I'll have to think about whether I can find a way to meet her at a hotel.

What does it say about me that I'm jealous of Boo 'cause he gets to sleep with my woman?

Hey babe,

Just mentioning, incentivizing through reward works for me too. And if you'd like, I'll be happy to cuss out your mother to earn extra rewards.

Glad Thanksgiving ended on a high note. Your sister and her husband sound solid. It's encouraging to hear they're still "connected" after all the time they been together. I'm hoping the trait runs in the family.

I looked up that kickass SUV, and you're right, there's nothing like it. A giant toy for the rock star who has everything.

Let me know how the vid Frisbee lessons go. I have a feeling Boo will enjoy it once you get the hang of it. Sounds like he has a "special" friend in Eloise.

I'm guessing by now Max has chilled and is handling her new relationship. She's lucky to have you to smooth out the edges. I know how that feels. Sometimes, and I'm betting you don't know you're doing it, you say the exact right thing to make me feel better. I'm sure your skills have been honed by your profession, but that's simply a case of polishing the raw material. You have that in you, the ability to make people feel better about themselves.

Enjoy Andie's show. I'm sure it will be great.

I don't want to miss saying this on time. Merry Christmas, baby. You're the best present a man could ever want or need. Next year, I promise. I'll make it up to you.

Ross

Dutchford, CT
Theresa
Nowhere Near Enough

Max has taken a powder. I call her the Monday after my spa day turned into a sleep-a-thon spa weekend. I want to discuss what I'd learned about who owns the company my dad manages, and what that might mean about the brothers' breakup. Max doesn't answer. Over the next few days, I call her fifteen times. I run her to ground. I dig deep, but she's nowhere to be found. I call the salon where she works, and all her boss, an eccentric woman named Bernadette, knows is that Max called in and said she needed an emergency vacation, and she'd be back in a week. Lola can't reach her and she's freaking out, which, in the middle of Lola's nausea-filled pregnancy, is not a good thing. Ziggy doesn't know where Max is, but Ziggy only cares where Max is when Ziggy needs Max, and right now, Ziggy is still pissed at Max. And me. She hung up on me after telling me, "You and Max can fuck right off."

Charming as always.

After Lola and I talk, she calls her husband, the new lieutenant at the Redwood Falls police department, and asks him if he could put out an APB for Max's car. She calls me back and shares that he told her there was no reason to do that because Max had called her boss and said she was taking an emergency vacation. There's nothing to indicate foul play.

That statement put Lola into action, and she uses her key to let herself into Max's apartment, which is in Lola's words, "Neat and tidy until I hit the bedroom, where it looked like a category five tornado had rolled through."

I know what this is about. Max is running away from that guy who she's fallen for. I ask Lola if she knows who the guy is, and Lola says, "I didn't know she was seeing anyone. She never said a word."

Back to Bernadette, who, I surmise, might know more than she's letting on. But after grilling her for ten minutes, Bernadette, who's pissed Max hadn't informed her she was dating someone, doesn't know jack shit about who that someone might be.

Now I'm worried about Max, and I want answers about my father.

For the ten thousandth time today, I wish I could pick up the phone and call Ethan. He'd know what to do to find Max. Even if he didn't, talking to him about it would make me feel better. I don't know if I've pouted since I was five years old, but I sit in my office pouting because I want Ethan, and I want him now.

Nope. Nothing adult going on here at the moment.

When my receptionist buzzes me to let know my next patient has arrived, I put petulant Theresa away, rearrange my face, and make sure Dr. Calapiano is on duty.

After my patient leaves – a lovely nineteen-year-old who doesn't know how to say no to her asshole boyfriend – I bite my lower lip and decide I have to do what I have to do to get answers.

I pick up the phone and call Don Alessandro Di Caro.

***

Of course, I bring him a Christmas present, which took me three days to find. I know he doesn't need them, but the platinum cufflinks with two small sapphires in the bottom corner are elegant, like he is, and they're understated, which he appears to be, but isn't.

I push the little box wrapped in shiny silver paper across the table at the newest Japanese restaurant to open in Dutchford. "Merry Christmas."

"Theresa. This is unexpected and thoughtful. Thank you." He slips the box into his suit-jacket's pocket. "Merry Christmas to you too."

I smile. "Thank you for meeting me." Again, I'm struck by the resemblance between him and his son. Gio is nearly a mirror image of his father.

"My pleasure. Anytime." We open our menus, and he asks, "What's good? I know you're our resident foodie."

He's smooth. I'll give him that. "I like the Bento boxes. You get a little of a lot of things, and that satisfies without making you feel stuffed."

"Sounds appealing." He spends another minute browsing, then puts down the menu. "How are you feeling?"

With him there are no half-truths or prevarications since he seems to know everything you're going to say anyway. "Sometimes the scar pulls, but that's rare now. My breathing is no longer impaired, but I won't be running the Boston Marathon. My endurance will always be compromised." His amazing blue eyes seem steelier. "But, overall, my doctors say I've made a remarkable recovery, due in no small part to the excellent care I received because of you."

He dips his chin not even in a full nod. "I'm relieved to hear you're doing so well. However, the medical professionals did the work. I can't take any credit for your return to good health, but thank you."

That means that part of the conversation is over. Don Alessandro does modest really well. I move to a safer topic. "I spoke to Sofia yesterday. She seems to have an endless supply of energy and sounds like she's on top of the world."

"She's happy and is challenged. She was right. The Tufts program was the right choice."

I let out a little laugh. "You know I know you wish she would've waited longer to be married and get pregnant."

His lips twitch. "Parents' ideas of what is best for their children is not always in line with what their children think is best for themselves. In this case, I'll admit to having, shall we say, misgivings, but she chose a good man who will be the kind of husband I wished for her."

"He will be. She's his sun."

Now he smiles. "As I said, a good choice."

I've never been shy with Don Alessandro, and I wasn't going to start now. "Did you send Sofia to me? Was I your choice to be her therapist?"

If he's surprised or expecting the question, I'll never know. He's perfected the blank expression. Not even his blink response gives him away. "No. I had nothing to do with who she chose."

Great big mental sigh. That would've been a cloud hanging over our relationship I don't want. "Good to know. I want it to be something she did for herself."

"Of course you would. Without her making that first step, her recovery would have been compromised."

I squint. "Did you get a PhD I don't know about?"

He chuckles. "Lived a few years more than you. As they say, the school of hard knocks."

I don't think anybody has "hit" him in any way that word can be applied since he was a little kid. And maybe not even then.

I want answers, but I don't want to offend him. "This is a hard question, but it's important to me."

"Please, ask."

"Did you pay for all those medical bills as a favor to my father?"

For a fleeting moment I swear I see the *Ah* in his eyes. He hadn't known why I'd asked him to lunch. Apparently, my father hadn't shared.

"No, Theresa. Not at all. You are aware that we are able to sit here and discuss Sofia's full and happy life because of *you*. You took a bullet for *my* daughter. There is nothing I wouldn't do for you."

Well, shit. There's blue fire in his eyes. He absolutely means every word he said.

"I'm not being humble when I tell you it was instinct to protect her."

"And I thank God for you every day."

The waiter comes to the table, and we both order tea and Bento boxes. The Don's differs from mine in its absence of any fried foods. No surprise there. He doesn't look this good at his age – I'm guessing mid-fifties – by being careless with his eating habits.

"Last question."

He nods. Once.

"I'll preface this by saying, I didn't know Substantial Food Imports was your company until Thanksgiving." I pause not because I'm afraid to ask, but now I'm not sure I want to hear the answer. "How did you come to hire my father?"

Without hesitation he says, "We had mutual acquaintances in the food industry."

Well, that's open-ended.

"Did you know why he was looking for a job?"

"So not the last question."

"A follow-up."

"I'm not avoiding the answer, but I think it's best you talk to him about that. It's not my place to say."

The Don and I put our napkins on our laps as our tea and miso soup arrive.

I want to remind him that not two minutes ago he said he'd do anything for me, but that's churlish, and he's right. It's not his place to say. This is family business. My family's business, and I'm going to get to the bottom of it. I see another trip to Avon in my near future.

Over lunch we talk about how I'm building my practice back up, and he tells Christmas decoration stories that have me laughing. He pays for lunch, of course, and after we put on our coats, he grasps my upper arms, and then he bends down and kisses one cheek, the other, then back to the first.

As he turns to go, I grab his hand and say, "Thank you. Truly."

He nods once, gives my hand a light squeeze, then walks away. Tommy, who has been sitting at a table in the front by the window, gets up and steps in front of his Don, then holds the door open as he heads outside into a typical drizzly, gray, late fall Connecticut day.

***

Early in the evening I call my dad on his cell. I don't want to go to Avon. I don't want to talk to him in that house. It reminds me of a giant mausoleum.

"Hey, Dad."

"Is everything all right, honey?"

"Yeah. Sure. We didn't have much time together on Thanksgiving, and I thought we could meet for lunch on Saturday."

He doesn't say anything for a couple of beats. "Only you and me?" he asks.

"Yep. Father daughter time. We haven't done that for years."

He seems to warm to the idea. "Sure. Pick the spot, text me, and I'll meet you there at 12:30 on Saturday."

Which is what I do.

When the weather's nice, Dad plays golf on Saturday mornings, and goes into the office for a few hours in the afternoon. Mid-December does not lend itself to golf in the Northeast. Dad goes into the office on Saturday mornings, and in the afternoons, he and my mother play bridge in a large round-robin group that meets in the clubhouse – re-purposing after golf season – which culminates in a tournament. For my mother, bridge is a contact sport. Making it to the quarterfinals is akin to being first runner-up in Miss America. Respectable, but no one remembers you. Getting to the semifinals is winning Miss America, and making it into the finals is winning the Olympics. So far, my parents have made it to the quarterfinals, and that's nowhere near close enough to the gold for my mother.

My father couldn't care less. He'd play just to play. He likes the game, it makes my mother happy, and gives her something to focus on that's not him.

Since I know he's coming from his office in Hartford, I pick a Mediterranean place in West Hartford for lunch. My dad's not a picky eater, but he tries to stay away from heavy food.

I'm waiting at our table when he walks in. Laura favors our father. He's a little taller than average height, a shade over five-ten, is lean and has the angular good looks of a northern Italian. His family comes from the Monferrato region in Piemonte. Lots of comingling with the Swiss and the Germans went on back in the day, and you can see it in my father's reddish-brown hair, fair complexion, and light green eyes. My sister has those eyes, and my father's coloring, but her hair is dark brown, which comes from our mother's side of the family. Laura's about five-four. Shorter than average, but not tiny like me. I barely scrape five-one.

Dad leans down and gives me a kiss on the cheek. "A happy surprise, *cara*. We haven't done this in a while."

I feel guilty knowing I'm going to ambush him, but I figure that can wait until after we do the family chitchat.

He drapes his jacket around the back of the chair, then sits, rubbing his hands. The waiter comes over and Dad orders coffee, and I ask for herbal tea. Before I even get to ask how he's doing, he says, "I know you're chomping at the bit to ask me about Substantial and Alessandro, and I've spent the week thinking that now is as good a time as any to tell you and Laura, so if you wait a few minutes, she should be here soon. I don't want to repeat myself, and I figure it's better to get all the questions in at once."

Yep. My father is not dumb and never has been. As the waiter is putting Dad's coffee in front of him, Laura walks in, sees us, and begins to unwind her long, knit scarf from around her neck while heading toward the table. After the hugs and kisses are over, she orders a coffee and looks at me. "Were you going to tell me?"

"I didn't know if Dad was going to talk to me about it. He put me off at Thanksgiving, so I didn't have high hopes. I didn't want to get you riled up for no reason."

Laura smacks her knee. "When did I become so fragile?"

Dad laughs. "You know, I miss this. I really do. You two going at it at the dinner table, in the kitchen, by the pool. It didn't matter where in the house I was, I always heard you girls butting heads. I'm telling you now, Laurie, when Val and Austen start in on each other, let 'em. You both drove your mother crazy. Such strong, smart girls who knew their mind since you were little. Most of the time your mother wanted to referee or silence you, but I wouldn't let her. And I was right. Look at you now."

Well, that shut us up and good.

"Daddy." Laura reached out and squeezed his hand.

I smiled watching them, and when Dad turned his attention to me, he said, "I always knew it would be you who got to the bottom of this. Small, but scrappy. I used to tell your mother nothing could stop you." He leaned forward and whispered, "I was right about that too. Nothing has."

I know he means the shooting. I'll regret that until the day he dies, he'll always see me lying in a hospital bed fighting for my life. I make a promise to myself. I'm going to see him more often, and I'm going to do everything in my power to give him as many good memories as I can in the hope that they'll shove the bad memories into a small corner of his mind.

The waiter comes over and we order. When he comes back with pita bread, hummus, and olives, we dig in like starving wolves. As our blood sugar settles, my father sits forward and puts his elbows on the table. Something that would make my mother crazy. Dad wouldn't care about that either. He grew up working hard alongside his father, and while he enjoys a comfortable life now, in his mind, he's still a guy with dirt under his fingernails.

He has our attention when he begins with, "As you can imagine, this is a complicated story. Nothing as important as this is ever simple. I'm going to ask you to wait until I'm done before you bombard me with questions. All right?"

Laura and I nod, and she says, "Sure, Dad."

The waiter brings our food, but we wait for Dad to start.

"Your mother grew up poor. Dirt poor. You didn't know her parents. Her father died when she was six, and her brothers were ten and twelve. Your uncle Lorenzo became head of the family before he was even a teenager. Ren made sure Stefano and your mother went to school, but he started working as a day laborer in the fields. Back then there were a lot more farms around Santa Rosa, and the child labor laws weren't enforced the way they are now. Your grandmother took in washing and mending, and she baked bread. As you can imagine, they scraped by. As Ren got older, he took higher paying jobs, and for a while things were better. But in Stefano's last year of high school, their mother died. The way Ren described how she declined, she must've had cancer, but since they never went to doctors, they don't know what killed her."

Dad stops and tucks into his calamari. Laura and I glance at each other, then eat a little too. After a few minutes, he stops eating, wipes his mouth with his napkin, drinks a little water, then resumes.

"Ren made your uncle Stefano finish school. But Stefano was angry, sad, and angry he was sad. He joined the Marines, and was stationed at Camp Pendleton, except for the year he was in Okinawa. Your mother was fourteen when her mother died, and Ren was the only 'parent' she had. He worked seven days a week to keep a roof over their head, food on the table, and your mother in new clothes because he knew girls could be mean about that stuff. I met your mother at a party in Santa Rosa. She had just graduated high school and had begun working as a receptionist for a paint company. I took one look at her and knew she was the girl for me." He stops and laughs.

"What?" Laura asks.

"Your Uncle Ren wasn't as sure about that as I was. Dominic and I started the Redwood Falls Winery when he was twenty-two and I was twenty. We didn't have a pot to piss in, and if it wasn't for our father, we would've fallen flat on our faces more times than I can count. Needless to say, Ren wasn't impressed. But by the time I met your mother, the winery was surviving, and when Ren came up and saw the vineyards, he started to loosen up. I was twenty-five when I married your mother and she was nineteen. I took her away from everything she knew. Especially Ren. She loved me, and compared to the life she'd led, my family was rich. She was self-conscious for a long time, and worried she didn't measure up."

Well, that explains a helluva lot.

Typical of Laura, she says what I'm thinking. "No wonder," she says.

"No wonder what?" Dad asks.

"She's so attached to things."

Dad sighs and nods. "It certainly contributes, yeah."

We go back to eating for a while, and I see my Uncle Ren in a whole new light. He's a successful businessman who owns five gas stations in Santa Rosa, but talk about humble beginnings and dedication to family.

As if my dad hears my thoughts, he says, "After your mother and I got married, Ren got his high school equivalency, kept working two jobs seven days a week, but went to community college at nights. He'd saved enough money to work one job, night shift, and go to Sonoma State during the day where he got his degree in business. I never doubted Ren would be successful."

Most of this Max had shared with me and Laura, but still, our Uncle Ren is one impressive dude.

"Stefano left the Marines after seven years, took a trip around the world, met your

Aunt Asta, and brought her back to Santa Rosa and married her. Then he got a job at Northrop Grumman, and is still there. In other words, life went on, and your mother became more settled. She had you girls, and the winery was taking off."

Our waiter cleared away the plates, and Dad orders baklava for us to share.

"In nineteen-ninety, we started having food pairings with our wine tastings. Mostly local restaurants, creameries, and cheese producers worked with us. But we used a food importer in San Francisco to bring in Italian salami and a few other products. That's when I met Alessandro Di Caro."

Don Di Caro did not lie, but he sure didn't put a fine point on it either.

"Part of my job was procurement, and he did business with the guy who owned the food import company in San Francisco. Looking to expand his reach, Alessandro came out to the winery one weekend when we were having a big wine and cheese pairing event. He was impressed with what he saw, and asked if he could tour our father's vineyards.

"Your *nonno* loved Alessandro. As you know, Ter, he's a charming man with laser focus. But with your *nonno*, Alessandro was total old school. They talked only in Italian, and shared stories about home. Dad had never been to Sicily and loved hearing Alessandro's stories. Alessandro knew Piemonte well, and had done business with one of our cousins, which thrilled Dad."

Dessert arrives and it's a good thing there's three of us, because I could only manage one forkful. That stuff is sweeeet.

"Over the course of about eighteen months, Alessandro came out to visit us about four times. Your mother thought he was gracious and respectful. I liked him because he was straightforward and didn't hide his intentions. Your Aunt Asta and Uncle Stefano were at the winery for an event one of the times Alessandro was there, and they liked him." Dad laughs. "Especially your Aunt Asta. After he left, she couldn't stop talking about his blue eyes."

I chuckle. "His son, Gio, is a carbon copy. But if it's possible, he's even better-looking. I've been out with him and his fiancée, and girls, women, older women, all look at him like he's an ice cream cone they want to lick."

Laura says, "She ain't lying, Dad."

He smiles. "Your *nonna* commented on those blue eyes too." We all laugh. "Anyway, your *nonno* was in his early seventies at the time of Alessandro's last visit, when he made it clear he wanted to buy into the winery and the vineyard. Dad was all for it, and so was I. Dominic wasn't. He didn't want a Don to 'stain' the family."

Dad watched me closely before he continued. "We all knew there were two sides to Alessandro's businesses. I'm not a stupid or naïve man. I looked into his holdings, and saw they were straight up and well apart from the other side of Alessandro's businesses. I made sure the part of his organization he wanted to bring into the winery and the vineyard was clean. I brought the research to your Uncle Dominic, and I made him come with me to a couple of Bay Area businesses Alessandro had interests in. Dominic didn't care. He wanted no part of Alessandro Di Caro."

Dad folds his napkin and throws it on the table. Here comes what caused the split.

"One night, we had a family meeting at the winery. Your *nonno* and *nonna*, Dominic and Merrie, me and your mother. Your *nonno* and *nonna* made their case for the influx of cash. Grapes and wine are a huge business in California. About one hundred fourteen billion dollars annually. As we've seen, a fire or a flood can wipe out towns, vineyards, and wineries overnight. It's smart business to have stable investors who can help keep a business running, and, if need be, have the cash to help in times of emergencies. Your *nonno* was an astute businessman. He knew we needed strong backup to keep healthy. When he was done, everyone else said their piece. Merrie, as always, listened, and was quiet and thoughtful when she spoke. The only one who was against Alessandro's buy-in was your uncle.

"We had a rule. Major decisions had to be unanimous. As much as I thought my brother was being a horse's ass, if he didn't want to do it, I would've gotten back to Alessandro and told him no."

Dad shook his head and grimaced.

"Your mother pointed out that if what Dominic was afraid of was true, Alessandro could've or would've strong-armed us. That's when my brother turned ugly and said disparaging things to your mother about how someone with her background would recognize low class and excuse it."

Dad's lips have gone thin and his hands are fist-balls. My guess, he's sugarcoating what Dominic said. I know my uncle, and he has a temper and a sharp tongue. That night, he was the only one on the losing side of what sounds like a smart business play. I bet he lashed out, and chose the weakest person at the table to pick on.

"Your mother got upset and ran out of the winery, crying. It had been raining and she slipped and fell down." Dad looks at the ceiling. "She was bleeding." He closes his eyes." She was pregnant, and she was bleeding." He shakes his head and his eyes remain shut. "I took her to the hospital, but there was nothing they could do."

Dad gets up and walks toward the archway where the restroom signs are.

Laura and I have tears in our eyes.

"Holy shit," she says.

"Yeah," I say.

We reach under the table and clasp each other's hands and hold on tight.

"Fucker," Laura says.

"That's why Dad didn't tell us. He wanted us to have our family. He knew we wouldn't be able to look Uncle Dom in the eye if we knew all this before we were adults."

"Do I get a free pass if I fly out there and punch him in the face?"

God, I love my sister and her passion.

"I'm okay with it. Though I don't know that it'll help heal the rift."

Laura smiles. "You're the mistress of understatement. You know that, right?"

I grin.

Dad's heading back to the table and Laura and I release our hands.

Damn, I've never seen him so upset.

He sits and lifts his palm at us before we can say anything. "Let me finish. Then you can say what you have to say."

"Okay, Dad," I whisper.

"When Connie…your mother, came home, Dominic and Merrie were waiting for us. Dominic was crying. I mean sobbing. He apologized and begged our forgiveness. We told him it wasn't his fault. What happened, it was a tragic accident. He couldn't get past it. Weeks went by and he was beating himself up. Drinking and crying. What happened was awful, but he made it worse by openly wallowing in it. If he couldn't let it go, he should've pretended until he got his shit together. I couldn't stand his guilt, and your mother felt like she was the reason Dom and I were ripping apart."

He pounds his fist on the table, shakes his head, and takes a deep breath.

"After four months of Dom spiraling nonstop, I went to Dad and told him Connie and I needed to get away. Make a new start. He understood, but he hated that we were leaving.

"The vineyard and the winery were all I knew. I would've never gone to work for another winery or vineyard, and I had no idea what I was going to do to feed my family. I knew Alessandro was expanding his food import business, so I called him and asked if he had any job openings. We sold the house in Redwood Falls and moved to Avon to the first house. You remember that house?"

We nod. Laura remembers it better than I do. We were there about five years.

"Alessandro Di Caro has been good to me. He gave me a job. Nothing else. Your mother and I paid for the move with the money we had from the sale of our house. We had enough money left over to put a down payment on our first house here, and we started our new lives."

Dad gives us a pointed look.

"He allowed me to learn a new business on his dime, and to pay him back for his kindness, I worked hard to grow that business into what it is today. I have no idea what he does outside of our business relationship, which is friendly and respectful. Everything about Substantial is one hundred percent legal and aboveboard. He's never asked me to do anything but run his company to the best of my ability."

Dad sits back and looks like he's bracing for an onslaught.

Then he says one more thing. "I want you girls to cut your mother some slack. She blames herself for uprooting our lives, and she clings to her things and her rules to keep from going off the rails. She'll never acknowledge any of this, and she won't talk to you about it. She doesn't talk to me about it. But she loves me with a ferocity I've never known. And she loves you. She's become so rigid with herself, it's hard for her to express her love. But I've known and loved her for nearly thirty-seven years, and I'm telling you, she loves you girls. She loves Baz. She knows he's a good man who adores her daughter and their children. Valeria and Austen are her treasures. If anyone can loosen her up, it's you two. For your old man, give it some effort."

Laura says, "Totally, Dad."

I bobble my head. "Absolutely."

He waits. Then he waits some more.

"That's it. No fifty questions?"

Laura says, "I think you and Mom were more generous than I would've been."

"How so, Laurie?"

"You let Ter and I go away every summer to be with your family."

"Honey, they're your family too. You need to know them, and they need to be in your life. None of that changes, no matter what happened between me and Dom."

When the waiter comes over to see if one of us finally paid the check, I notice it's us and only one other table with people that are left in the restaurant.

Dad's faster on the draw and drops his credit card into the envelope thingie.

"Do you think you and Dom will ever talk again?"

"There's my shrink," he jokes. "We talk. When Mom and I went to *Nonno*'s and *Nonna*'s funerals, we spent some time with Dom and Merrie. He calls on birthdays, our anniversary, and Christmas. I call on birthdays, their anniversary, and Easter. Sometimes one of us picks up the phone for no reason. Over the years the calls have become less strained. He's my brother. He fucked up, but I love him. No regrets, girls. Our lives are here, and I have no desire to go back. My heart aches for your mother, who has taken on weight she doesn't need to carry. But I can't fix that."

He stands. "I've got to go to the clubhouse. Bridge starts in half an hour and if I'm late, your mother will kill me." He smiles. "Come give your old man a hug."

"See you soon, Dad," I say into his chest.

"Look forward to it, Ter."

"I'll come by with Val and Austen tomorrow, and I'll bring donuts," Laura says as she holds him.

"Bavarian crème for me." He pulls back and kisses Laura on the cheek, then bends and does the same to me.

Laura and I stand by the door and watch him get into his car and drive away.

Then we wrap our arms around each other and cry.

Portland, Maine
Ethan
James Bond

The day before I leave for Portland, Benita scopes out a few buildings to find the right one for me to disappear into, head out the back to collect another car, and drive off without a tail. Yeah, the ditch will let those fucktards know I know I'm being followed, but there's no way we can let them tail me. Aside from the obvious that we don't want to blow our cover, they must never know about those brave girls coming forward.

We're getting closer to cinching the noose, and we have to stay sharp.

I drive my car to the front parking lot of a medical building that opens at six-thirty. My tail in the Camry is parked a couple of rows over, and I feel the Russian's gaze boring into my back as I walk into the lobby. I head behind the building where the medical staff parks, get in the car Benita left for me, and I take the back alley to the next cross street where I turn and head to the interstate.

At the satellite office, Agent Grandeau comes out to greet me and takes us to a conference room. Thea Grandeau is a statuesque middle-aged woman who has a wide smile and an open manner. She tells me she's originally from New Orleans, but went to the University of Maine, met her husband there, and they settled in Portland.

The girls arrive a half hour later nervous and wary. Thea's warmth calms them, and after she explains the process, she gets down to it. With a practiced ease she gets them to remember details they haven't shared before. Much of their story sounds familiar. It's like the Russians follow a script. When Thea is done, I give them my phone to each girl to scroll through the photos of the Russians, and to a one they positively ID the two men who tried to dope them in the club.

The net widens with Thea, her colleagues, and PDs statewide now in the know about the Russian crew and their purpose. As I'm getting ready to leave, my phone rings and it's one of the NYPD members of the NY JTFF. After going through the club, bar, and campus-related doping reports from the past six months, he has two where the descriptions of two guys tag-teaming the targeted girls match the Russians.

Thea takes me to a cubicle, where I get on a computer and conference in with Skip and tell him about the NY call, and what I learned here. Now that a pattern is coming clear, Skip agrees I should go to NY to join the agent who'll speak with the girls who filed those reports. Better than two hours ago, I know what I'm listening for, and what specifically to ask.

Before I shut down the computer, I check the J-Gestia Gallery website to find out when Andie's opening is, and see it's this Friday night. I call the NY JTTF agent and ask if we can talk to the girls on Friday, and he's fine with that, and tells me he'll set it up.

On my way out of Portland, I'm thinking about how my plan is coming together, noting it was no more than a fantasy until now. I drop off Flower's letter at the Portland post office, knowing I'll be seeing her before she gets it.

Friday night Theresa will in the same bed as I am, and I don't expect we'll be doing much sleeping.

New York City
Theresa
The Gift

It's definitely a schlep to get from Dutchford, Connecticut to New York City. First I have to drive to my sister's house – one hour – where Boo is staying with Eloise and our parents, who are babysitting Valeria and Austen for the weekend. We're staying in the city to see a show, visit a couple of museums, eat too much great food, and get in a little shopping. Laura, Baz, and I are taking a train from Hartford to New Haven – an hour – then we're taking Metro North to NYC – two hours. No way are we driving to NYC, especially not on a Friday ten days before Christmas.

In preparation to go to Andie's opening, I shuffled a couple of patients, and I'm ready to leave the house at ten in the morning with Boo in the backseat going back and forth window to window on his tether. Dogs and cars. Need I say more?

It's pandemonium at my sister's house, but the good kind. Laura's shouting last-minute instructions to our parents as she runs through the kitchen from the laundry room. Baz is braiding Val's hair while Austen is jumping up and down on the sofa chanting, "Me too. Me too."

Dad goes outside to move my luggage to the trunk of his car as he's chauffeuring us to the station. After fourteen thousand hugs and kisses good-bye, we get to the station and on the train with a moment to spare, which is a miracle.

After we're seated, Laura leans into Baz and closes her eyes. He wraps his arm around her shoulders and drops a kiss on her hair. Not three minutes later, she's asleep.

"She wants to return to work full time next year," he tells me. "Says she needs the quiet."

Laura is in a niche industry. She procures rare things for serious collectors. Mostly books, letters, and reading-related historical objects. Her workday is filled with nonstop phone calls that are interspersed with research and frenetic emailing. She's been able to keep her business going since Val was born, but at nowhere near the volume it was before becoming a mom.

"Last week," Baz says, "Austen answered Laura's phone and told one of her clients that mommy was in the bathroom doing what comes naturally." I laugh. "Sir Harold something-or-other told Austen to tell her mommy to call him after she was fully restored. It took Laura twenty minutes of listening to Austen repeat what she heard for Laura to decipher the message."

"Laura will get payback when she tells that story to Austen's boyfriends."

Baz scowls. "Austen won't have boyfriends until she's thirty."

"Good luck with that," I say while chuckling.

By the time we arrive at our hotel – SoHo boutique-y with a bit of earthy – we need a drink and a nap. We agree to meet in the lobby at seven to go for drinks and a light nosh before heading to the gallery. The opening reception starts at eight-thirty.

I've never been one to sacrifice comfort for fashion. That being said, tonight's a big night for Andie, and I know there are going to be a lot of "beautiful people" at the opening, lots of paps, cameras, and press.

With the mindset of I'm not going to let our side down, I'm wearing my new clingy cashmere sweater dress. It's ivory with long sleeves, a mock turtle collar, and basically no back – the scoop hits my waist. I put tons of conditioner and taming product in my hair, and blow it out to as straight as I can get it, then pull it back into a severe ponytail, and I wrap a hank of hair around the ponytail band and tuck it in. The effect is a dark brown column lying against bare skin.

I have on my over-the-knee tan suede boots with delicate crisscross lacing up the back. The heels are solid, not spikey, but they're high, over four inches, and I need the height more than ever tonight. Have you seen those six-foot models? They're gorgeous and in bare feet they have nearly a foot on me.

Dramatic eye makeup and light foundation to even out the tone, and deep cherry lipstick are highlighted by platinum chandelier earrings encrusted with garnets and diamond chips. No bracelets, but a large oval ruby surrounded by diamonds is on my right middle finger. I take one last look in the full-length mirror, then grab up my little black velvet clutch and drape my black velvet opera coat over my arm.

I arrive at the lobby first, and while I'm waiting next to a large plush sofa, a handsome man wearing an amazingly tailored suit approaches me, bends down, and whispers in my ear, "You look good enough to eat."

Before I have a chance to respond, he walks away – nice view there too – and exits the lobby.

Okay. As hit-and-run compliments go, that one works.

Laura and Baz come toward me and Laura and I do something we've been doing since we're little girls. We twirl for each other. Spinning around at least two times so each of us get the full effect of what we're wearing and how we look.

"Jesus, Ter," Laura breathes out. "You plan on making someone fall in love with you tonight?"

"Gotta say," Baz adds, "you're smokin'."

Between the anonymous compliment and their approval, I preen a little. It's been a long time since I had this. In March it will be two years since I was shot, and being in New York City and looking good is an ego boost I'm definitely enjoying.

"Well," I return, "dapper as always, Baz." He's wearing a black turtleneck flat knit sweater, black trousers, a camel hair blazer, and black boots. His dark hair is "lightly salted" and he looks urbane and erudite.

Laura is a vision in a dark green jacquard silk wraparound dress. She's wearing all fifteen varying lengths diamonds-by-the-yard necklaces Baz has given her each year on their anniversary. Her small diamond pave half-hoop earrings were this year's birthday present. She's always been a looker, and while she's become curvier since having the girls, she still has the body of a college student.

"Wow, Laurie. Absolutely beautiful." I look down at her dark green spikey pumps. "Where did you find those?"

"Maude's."

Maude's is a small boutique buried in the country near Laura's house. If you don't know where it is, you'll never find it, but Maude does a brisk business.

"Figures."

"Since we pass muster, let's get some food and alcohol in our bodies, not necessarily in that order."

Coats, scarves, and gloves are donned, and we walk two blocks to a bistro and have martinis, mini crab cakes, mushroom wontons drizzled with truffle oil, and baked panko-encrusted spinach and fontina rice balls. Before we leave, Laura and I go to the bathroom, and then check each other and then the mirror to make sure we don't have spinach in our teeth. After lipstick reapplication, we join Baz and walk three blocks – I'm so glad I'm wearing these boots, it's freezing out – to the gallery.

As expected, there's a ton of people milling on the sidewalk, most with cameras, some with phones. Everyone's trying to get a snap of the celebrities, and someone famous is entering as we make it to the outer edge of the crowd. The paps are yelling, "Dara, Dara, this way."

"You think they mean Dara Banalista?" Laura asks.

"She didn't call to tell me she was coming," I shrug, "but I'm guessing, yeah."

Laura smacks my arm. "Smart-ass."

The entrance is cordoned off and two huge security guards are standing behind the red velvet ropes. We show our invitations to the guards, and one of them unhooks the rope to let us pass, and says, "You have to check in at reception when you're inside."

Reception is a huge curved indigo-veined white marble desk. The woman behind the desk is a work of art all by herself. Deborah Harry-esque white-blonde hair in a classic blunt cut, her bright blue eyes are rimmed in thick kohl. That's it. No other makeup. Not that she needs it. She has a narrow face with a high forehead, sharp cheekbones, and full wide lips covered in nude lipstick. She's wearing a one-piece body-clinging white jumpsuit, with a thick silver zipper that goes from her crotch to her chin.

We hand her our invitations, and in a deep, silky voice she says, "Names please." We oblige and she taps her iPad, scrolling through a long list. "Which one of you is Theresa?"

"Me," I say.

She hands an envelope to me, then, like a ballerina, her arm drifts out to her side to indicate we can go in. "Enjoy the show," she purrs.

As we walk around the black matte false wall I'm guessing is there to keep the paps' flashes from interrupting the show, Baz says, "That alone was worth the trip."

Laura looks up at him and grins. Then she turns to me. "What's with the envelope?"

"I have no idea, but after we hand over our coats," I tilt my head toward the cloakroom on the left, "I'll let you know."

As the incredibly beautiful young man in all black takes our coats, and as we wait to get our little tags, I turn to face the gallery. The hum of hundreds of conversations warms an otherwise stark white room with forty-foot ceilings. What would be a cavernous space is filled with people standing around twenty-five larger than life-size sculptures of couples, always couples, that's Andie's thing and signature. Each couple, some two males, some two females, some male and female, are in various states of undressing, and all are kissing, but not necessarily on the mouth. Somehow, she's able to capture the beauty of emotion in stone, and that's where her talent lies – the sculptures look like real people frozen in time.

Barely visible through the crush is a long white linen-covered table filled with food flanked by bars on either side. Baz says, "I'm headed that way." He indicates a bar, then slips the young man some money as he hands over our tags.

I ask him, "Where's the ladies' room?" and he points to a small hallway around the corner from the cloakroom. I say, "Thanks," then tell Laura and Baz, "Go. Drink. Mingle. I'll find you."

They nod and head into the fray as I make my way to a quiet space to see what's in the mysterious envelope.

The bathroom is all cement except the stall doors, the toilets, and the faucets over the trough-like sink that runs under the sink-to-ceiling wall-to-wall mirror.

There are a couple of stunning women who look like models standing by the padded cement bench, but this is New York, so who knows if they're models or stockbrokers. I don't want to intrude on their conversation, and stand next to the sink with my clutch tucked under my arm. The envelope feels like it has a credit card in it and a piece of paper. I tear open the side of the envelope and a hotel room cardkey drops into my hand. On its face is a picture of a sofa and seating arrangement in what looks like a hotel lobby, and the name of the hotel is written across the top, and the address and phone number is written across the bottom.

Way weird, and this is giving me the heebie-jeebies. I don't know this hotel, but I know where it is: off Central Park on the

Upper West Side. I drop the cardkey back in the envelope and pull out the piece of paper that is folded in half. I open it and the hotel's name is embedded in the top of the paper. Strong, masculine writing:

Hey babe. I'm waiting. Room 623.
Ross

I gasp and clutch the lip of the sink to hold myself up.

He's here.

In New York City.

Waiting for me at a hotel.

I can't seem to take enough air into my lungs and I'm almost panting.

One of the two women who were by the bench and are now leaning over me says, "Are you all right?"

I nod but tap my chest.

"Do you have asthma? Is there an inhaler in your bag?"

"I'm…I'm…fine. Really. Had a bit of a shock, that's all."

They look down to the envelope and the other woman asks, "Do you want us to call someone for you?"

My breathing is evening out and I say, "It's a good shock. Honestly." I can't help the smile that I feel spreading across my face. "Total surprise, though. Never expected it."

The smile must give away the gist of my reaction. They smile back, and one says, "Happy for you."

The other nods and says, "Sounds like you're going to have a good evening."

Now I'm grinning like an idiot. "The best."

They nod and head out of the bathroom as three women head in. I put the note back in the envelope and put it in my clutch.

Now I have to explain this to Laura in a way that she'll be happy for me without asking three hundred questions.

Before I hunt down my sister, I look to where the biggest crowd is gathered and see Andie and Lars standing with people and having their picture taken. The people say a few words to Andie and Lars, then move away, and another few people come forward for a photo. I move as close as I can get to watch the shift of people then a photo repeat. And repeat. No way I'm going to be able to say hello to Andie and congratulate her.

As I turn to walk away, Lars shouts out, "Ter."

I see him waving me over, and I cut through a few people who look at me like, *Why is she special?* as I make it to Lars and Andie and get giant hugs from each of them.

"An incredible accomplishment, Andie. Congrats."

She beams. "It's been a good show. Everything sold earlier this week through private viewings. So now it's all party-party all night long. Where's Laura and Baz?"

"Mingling. Drinking. Enjoying being adults."

"Excellent," Lars says. "Get 'em to come to say hey."

"Will do." I squeeze Andie's hand. "So happy for you."

She smiles. "Me too."

We do cheek pecks good-bye and I walk off and find Laura and Baz where I imagined they would be, standing near the bar with little munchies on napkins. They're talking to a couple I sort of recognize. Laura looks up, sees me, and hand flaps for me to come over. Easier said than done. The area is thick with people.

Finally, I make it to them and Laura says, "You remember our friends Cecil and Mae."

Right. Now I remember. Cecil is a professor at the same college as Baz, but Cecil's a scientist. I don't remember what kind. Mae's an artist. Paintings. Huge abstracts. She's friends with Andie. "Hi. It's been a minute."

"A couple of minutes. Two Christmases ago to be exact," Cecil says. "We were on sabbatical in South America. I was doing research." That's it. I remember now. His specialty is infectious diseases. "How have you been?"

They were gone when the shooting occurred, and my guess, Baz and Laura didn't share. "Well, thanks. Nothing as exciting as what you've been doing." Before he launches into their year in the jungle, I say, "If you don't mind, I need to steal Laura for a moment."

"Sure, sure," Cecil says.

I take Laura's hand and pull her to a pocket of relative quiet against a wall. Right away she asks, "Why do you look like you're about to break into song?"

Can't get anything by my sister. "Listen—"

"Oh boy. This is something big if you're starting with listen."

"Can I talk now?"

She rolls her eyes. "Go ahead."

"Listen first and don't *interrupt*." She glares. "I've been seeing someone." Her eyes bug out and she grabs my hand. "He's been on a work assignment but managed to get away and he's just arrived in the city." I'm winging it.

"The envelope."

"Yeah." More fabrication. "He wanted to make sure I got the message."

"So it would seem."

"I'm leaving to meet him, but I'll call you in the morning with an update."

"Holy shit. You're into him, like bigtime."

I smile. "Bigtime."

"Double holy shit. Is he the one?"

I nod.

"Are you his one?"

I blink. Slowly.

"Holy fuckin' shit."

I know that tone. The three hundred questions are lined up for launch. "Not tonight, Laurie. I don't think he's going to be here long, and I want as much time with him as I can get. I will tell you everything, I promise. But right now, I'm leaving. I saw Andie and Lars, and they told me they want you and Baz to go hang with them." I let go of her hand and give her a tight hug. "I'll call you in the morning."

My beautiful sister has tears in her eyes. "God. I've wanted this for you for so long. Go. Tell him we can't wait to meet him."

"I will."

I turn and push my way through a throng of people like a mini pile driver. I get my coat, then walk out onto the sidewalk and hail a taxi.

Ethan is a cab ride away.

***

Getting from SoHo to the Upper West Side takes way too long, even though I have a great cabbie who got us out of SoHo and onto what I think is called the West Side Highway pretty fast. Now we're off the parkway, going up Seventy-ninth Street, and my breathing is becoming a little erratic again.

Since the shooting, everything I've done has been measured. Recovery and therapy in the hospital. Rehab and therapy in the care center. Therapists coming to the house. Going for walks with Boo and playing in the park. All of it has been done in increments. A slow and steady progression to build up my lung capacity while giving my body time to heal in a way that would benefit me the most.

I've never had these kind of adrenaline rushes except when Ethan and I were going at it in the storeroom. I'd been breathy then, but nothing like this where it's become difficult to pull air into my lungs. I close my eyes and remember the exercises I'd been taught about visualizing my lungs expanding with each inhale and deflating with each exhale. Slowly, I can feel my lungs loosening, but now I'm worried I'll ruin what I hope will be nonstop sex.

I feel the taxi slowing, and I open my eyes. We stop in front of a lovely older building, maybe ten stories high, the kind you see all over New York City. There's a maroon awning over the entryway with the name of the hotel in white. I pay the cabbie, walk into the hotel, and I'm on a landing looking over the lobby, which has old-world charm. I walk down the steps, and take the cardkey out of my clutch in case the front desk people wonder who I am. I want to show them I belong there. I walk to the elevator and press UP. When it arrives, I'm alone when I step in and press 6. I have the sense I'm supposed to slip in unseen.

When the elevator stops, I walk out into a narrow hallway and look to see if anyone's around. Assured it's empty, I look up to the room number plaques to see which way I need to go. To the left, I go down the hall, make a right, and the room number is on the door at the end of this little hallway. My whole body is shaking and my hand is so unsteady I can't get the card in the slot. As I'm about to try again, the door flies open and Ethan picks me up and plants me in a small living room as he closes and double locks the door.

This is one of those moments where I wish for the superpower to slow down time. I want to take in every inch of him. His broad shoulders, his fine behind, those thick thighs, and… Whoosh, I'm off my feet again and in his arms.

"Baby, I've missed you," he whispers in my ear. "Give your man some sugar."

I move my head and take in the fire blazing in his fabulous blue eyes and just like that, he's my entire world. I open my mouth and lower my lips to his, and he touches the tip of my tongue with his, and we ignite. Gentle exploration is not happening here. We're going at each other full throttle. He tastes exactly as I remember, musky and fiery. I push my fingers into his hair and grab on as I drink him in, knowing I have to get enough to last me until he finishes with his op.

He pulls back and says, "Damn, baby. You taste so fuckin' good."

I smile and he lowers me, holding my arms until I'm steady on my feet.

My clutch is on the floor, my gloves next to it, and the envelope is lying across the clasp. He bends down and picks up my stuff and puts it on a desk behind me. When he turns around, he puts his hands under my coat onto my shoulders and I loosen my arms as he removes the coat and walks to the closet where he hangs it up. I turn to take in the room, and I feel his warm fingers dip beneath the bottom of the oval cutout. He rests his warm palm on my back.

"That's a lot of skin you're showing."

I understand that's code for this is mine and no one else gets to see it, but I know he's more enlightened than Neanderthal so I don't respond. Instead I turn and ask, "How long do we have?"

New York City
Ethan
All Mine

"Forever, baby. You're all mine for the rest of our lives."

She smiles and leans into me, putting her hand on my stomach when she says, "That works."

I want her so bad I don't know what to do first. But as much as I need *in there*, I've got to slow the fuck down. My heart is thundering in my chest and my brain is scrambled. I take her in, scanning her body from her sexy fuckin' boots to her sparkly earrings. She looks so beautiful it hurts. That dress – damn, that dress – is a homing signal for my dick. From the front it covers everything, but it clings to her body and shows off all her dips and curves. The back is an invitation. A big oval of nothing but skin. If I'm out with her when she's wearing something like that, I'll be throwing off, *Yeah, that's mine, and no, you'll never get close to that.* But when I'm not with her... Yeah, I'm a caveman, but she's a grown woman, and I don't get to tell her what to wear and where to wear it.

I lay my hand over hers. "I have to leave by nine tomorrow morning, babe."

"Well, that sucks."

"Yeah, it does."

She turns around and I guess she's taking in the room. It's a small suite with a living room and bedroom. French doors separate the two rooms. I chose the hotel because it's small and old, and they don't have cameras on each floor, only at the front desk. Their lack of security significantly minimizes the chance anyone would see into which room she went. I paid for the room in cash and used "Nick's" credit card to secure the incidentals. Since there won't be any, there'll be no trace of my stay.

To make sure no one followed her to the room, I ask, "Were you alone in the elevator coming up?"

"Yep. And there was no one in the hallway when I got off the elevator."

My woman is smart, but I hate that she even has to think about that shit. "Good."

She takes a step back, turns, and flips her long ponytail over her shoulder. "Unbutton me, Ethan."

No argument. She wants me in there as bad I want in there, and that's another reason she's made for me. She's not shy. She wants it, and she has no problem letting me know. Perfect.

There are three buttons on the neck held in place with little loops. As I stare at the slope of her neck and her bare back, I run my hands over the front of her body, molding my hands around her small, tight, braless tits, then rub my thumbs over her nipples only once, and right away they pebble into hard nubs. She moans and writhes in my arms.

Christ, she's so responsive.

I skim my hands down to her stomach, then to her waist, where I circle my hands. I let them rest on her body, which I feel vibrating beneath my touch. I move my hands back to cup her juicy ass, and I squeeze the globes. Damn, this material feels great, but nowhere near as smooth and flawless as the skin on her back where I press my lips below the dress's neckline. Then, gently, 'cause those loops are delicate, I unhook each button. When the neck releases, she turns and backs up a few steps as I watch her tug the sleeves until the top of the dress falls, leaving her naked from the waist up.

Oh shit. She's standing there waiting to see my reaction to the half-inch-wide scar that runs from below her collarbone to the top of her rib cage. I'm guessing, aside from medical personnel, I'm the first man to see her scar, and she has to be worried it'll turn me off.

It's better I show her rather than tell her that scar is a badge of honor. I don't know a single person who would've done what she did. She's a walking fucking miracle.

"Come here, baby."

She walks to me on those sexy-as-hell boots and stops until there's almost no space between us. I sink to my knees, wrap my arms around her thighs, and proceed to place soft kisses on the bottom of the scar. Slowly, I kiss my way up until I can go no farther.

I feel the sob before it escapes. I angle her waist until she understands and allows me to pull her down until I'm holding her against my chest. Softly, she cries, and I cradle her to me, this precious woman who is more warrior than anyone I know.

"That scar is as much a part of you as your smile, baby. I love it all, and you never have to worry that I'll find it to be anything but what it is, a symbol of your strength."

She lifts her head, and I wipe away the wet on her face. No ugly crying for my woman. Her face is as pretty as the moment I first saw her in Boston when she was laughing.

I put one arm under her knees and the other around her back and she stops me. "Beside you. We do this and everything side by side."

"Okay, baby."

I stand and offer her my hand, which she takes. Then she steps back and grabs the hem of the dress and pulls it over her head. Holy hell. Not only is she braless, but she's not wearing panties or pantyhose. She's got on lace-topped thigh-highs and those boots, which come to a couple of inches above her knee. I see some sheer stocking, white lace, and healthy munchable thighs.

"Don't take off another thing," I order.

She grins, then walks her sweet, full ass into the bedroom, then stands at the end of the bed waiting for me.

I pull my sweater over my head and unbuckle my belt as I toe off my boots. I walk to her and say, "First I'm going to have you on your back, and those legs with those fuckin' boots are going to be over my shoulders. Then I'm going to fuck you from behind so I can watch that fantastic ass while I'm taking you. After that, it's lady's choice."

She's breathing heavy when she rasps out, "Okay."

I pull the strip of condoms out of my front pocket and toss them on the bed, then I push my pants and briefs down and my socks go with them.

She gasps, and then moans, and I have to say, I'm all kinds of rooster. God has been good to me in a lot of ways. Making sure my equipment matches my proportions is one of them.

Simultaneously, we pull down the bedding, exposing the sheets. She climbs onto the bed, lies back and crooks her legs open, and I know I have to deviate from my announced plan. That's one pretty pussy, and I want to take an up-close look before I taste what's mine.

I called it. Being Flower is part of her. She tastes like what sweet flowers smell like, and I can't get enough. Lapping at her, nibbling on her clit, I have to hold her hips since she's dancing horizontally on the bed while moaning loud. I smile as I'm eating her, knowing I'll have thousands of opportunities to make her writhe before I make her come.

She's pounding the bed with her fists as I suck her clit, and when she explodes, it's spectacular. She's pulling my hair and screaming my name. Repeatedly.

I could win every lottery in America, and it wouldn't even touch how amazing her reaction makes me feel.

After she comes down, and I've licked up every drop of her nectar, I rip off a condom packet, tear it open, and roll that fucker on. Then I grab her legs, throw them over my shoulders, and slide into *my* pussy, knowing I've found heaven on earth.

Christ, she's so tight and so tiny. I'm afraid I'm going to hurt her.

Her hands are anchored on my hips and we're staring into each other's eyes. "I'm yours," I tell her.

"I'm yours," she whispers back.

Slowly, I start to stroke, and I keep a steady rhythm, feeling her tight channel flex around me. She's meeting my thrusts and her fingers are digging into my ass.

"Ethan," she calls. I keep stroking. "Ethan," she says my name louder. "Ethan, look at me." I stop, feeling the sweat that's beaded up all over my body.

It's been a while since I've been with a woman, and this is not any woman. Theresa is my woman, and I want her in every way I can have her with an intensity I've never felt before. Even though I got her off already, I'm not going to slam-bam-thank-you-ma'am her. Not now, and not ever. This woman, *my* woman, deserves better.

I'm gazing at her sweet face. Her pupils are dilated, and her cheeks are flushed.

"Let go, honey." She squeezes my ass. "I'm not made of glass. Go ahead and let go."

I want it to last, but her pussy is so fuckin' tight. I'm at the end of my control and she's giving me permission to ride her hard.

"It's so good, baby. I wanna blow right now."

"So blow. Take all you want, as much as you want, however you want it. I'll be right here waiting for more."

The light in her golden-brown eyes is dancing, and I know I'll be driving back to Connecticut tomorrow morning with zero sleep.

***

After hours of the most energetic, fuckin' fantastic sex of my life, Theresa is lying in my arms clinging to me after telling me the story of her father, his brother, and Alessandro Di Caro. She explained why she didn't say anything in her letters, telling me she's being mindful of my position. "I would never put anything about a Don in a letter," she says.

Here, in the early hours of the morning, before the light of day has broken, she has shared deep personal stories about herself and her family, and once again, I'm humbled she loves and trusts me.

"You should know," she says, "I told Laura I have a man, and he's 'the one.'"

"Well, I fuckin' hope so."

She laughs and tugs my earlobe. "She and Baz can't wait to meet you."

"I can't wait to meet them, your folks, your crazy cousins, your nieces, and Boo. I can't wait until you meet Trask and his family, and my mom and dad. I want to take you to Fiddler's Rest. I want to go to California and meet the rest of your family. I want it all, baby. You. Your family. My family, and most of all, our family."

She's leaning on my chest, running her fingers through my chest hair, her nails zinging straight to my dick. We've fucked all night. How my dick is even working right now is a wonder.

"How many?" she asks.

"How many what?"

"How many kids you want?"

Theresa and my kids. The thought of it gut punches me. "At least two. You?"

"Two or three. Depending on whether we get one of each with two, or we have to keep going."

"Let's say three since I'd like to see your smile on as many faces as we can make."

She lifts up and touches her lips to mine. "Three then." She pokes me in the chest. "You better finish up this case soon. I'm nearly thirty-two, and if we're having three kids, we need to get on that soon."

"I want some time with you first. We're okay for a couple of years before we start making babies. I want to have you all to myself for a while."

"Well, when you put it like that." She throws her leg over my hips – the boots are gone, but those thigh-highs are staying right where they are – and sits on me. I'm already hard. She starts rubbing her pussy against my dick, making herself wet.

"Get it, babe." I grab her ass, but don't stop her motion. "Take what you want."

I'm watching the show and loving what I see. She doesn't hold anything back, everything she's feeling is written all over her face.

And I'm her "one." Amazing.

Her hands are on my pecs and her nails are digging into my skin as she's working herself up. She stops, leans over, grabs the much shorter strip of condoms, pulls one off, and scooches back a bit as she tears the foil. I lift my dick to help her, and she grins as she rolls the condom slowly down to the root.

As she takes me inside, she's holding her bottom lip with her teeth. I sit up and take that luscious lip between my teeth, then soothe it with my tongue. She wraps her legs around me, and we begin to kiss, slow and deep. She's grinding on me, gripping me with her pussy's inner walls, moaning down my throat as she works that spot deep inside her.

This is different than our sex-a-thon, which was all about exploring and satisfying needs and fantasies we'd been harboring for months. This is about our connection. Our bodies saying what we know is true: we love each other. We found our forever.

Slowly, she's building it in me, and herself, and when she moves her hands from my cheeks, she circles my shoulders, I can feel she's almost there. We're pressed so tightly together, her moves become mine. She pulls her head back, breaking the kiss so she can watch me as she lets go. I'm right there with her, my release a slow and steady rush.

"Love you, Ethan," she says, and she lowers her head to my shoulder.

"Love you, baby. So much."

**

She doesn't want me driving without sustenance. That's the word she uses. But she has to know she's fed my soul. Given me a well of reserves to draw on as I'm forced to face more time away from her. God, I can't wait for this fuckin' op to be over.

We're sitting naked in bed – she's still wearing the thigh-highs – eating breakfast, drinking coffee, and she's looking at houses on her phone.

"I'm thinking Framingham," she mutters, her head down, looking at the screen. "It's about twenty-six miles to your office."

"How far to Dutchford?"

Her head comes up. "About forty miles."

"Too far, Flower. It's dark at four o'clock all of December. I don't want you driving that far in the dark, especially in bad weather."

"But it's okay for you to drive that far in bad weather in the dark?"

I grin.

She sighs. "I'm not going to win this argument, am I?"

"Nope." I grab the phone, look at the map, then look up a few towns. When I hand the phone back to her, I point at the screen and say, "Mendon. It's six miles to the freeway, and then it's all freeway to the office." As she starts tapping, I add, "Forty miles. Freeway miles. Not winding two-lane-road miles. There's a difference, and you know it."

She shakes her head. "Your Neanderthal tendencies need tempering."

I laugh. "I'm sure you'll do your level best to work on that."

"Damn straight."

"Mendon, babe. Look it up. From the little I read, it's mostly homeowners, good schools, and more exurban than suburban." I take the phone from her hand, toss it on the bed. Then I put my hands under her armpits and lift her to her knees. She walks on her knees to me. "Find a house with a conservatory, enough land for Boo and kids to run around with space left over for your greenhouse."

With one hand she cups my jaw and with the other she runs her fingers through my beard while gazing at me. "You going to take a shower?" She's trying hard to stay level, but I can feel the sad descending on both of us.

"Nope. Wanna smell you on me for as long as I can."

"Hurts," she whispers.

I close my eyes and take a deep breath. When I open them, I see her fighting tears. "When this op is over, I'm going to ask if there are any openings in Intelligence. They do threat analysis and make strategic recommendations. With my background and language skills, I think they'll see me as an asset."

"Honey, you'll lose your mind being tied to a desk."

"I'm losing my mind being away from you." She touches her mouth to mine. "If I feel this way now, how am I going to feel when I'm away from you and our kids? I can't say to Skip, I'll remain a Special Agent only if you don't keep me away from my wife and kids for more than a couple of days."

She smiles. "I see your point." With one of her small delicate hands, she caresses my cheek. "You know your limits. I trust that. But I don't want you to regret anything. Regret can turn into resentment, and that would be awful for both of us."

"We'll talk more about it when the op is over. In the meantime, I'll explore my options."

"'Kay." She looks at the clock, and I follow her sightline.

Shit. It's eight-twenty. I down my coffee then say, "I'll use the bathroom first. I'm fast."

She nods, and I feel my jaw tighten.

I hate this.

She's dressed when I come out, and she grabs my hand and squeezes as she walks by to go into the bathroom.

Fifteen minutes later her head is lying below my pecs, and her arms are around my waist. I'm sifting my fingers through her soft hair, and I can't find the words to tell her any of it. How much she means to me. How much I love her pussy, ass, and thighs. How leaving her is ripping my heart out of my body.

I place my hands on her cheeks and lift her head. I lean down and kiss her deep, wet, and slow, trying to pour everything I feel for her into that kiss.

When I raise my head, she smiles up at me and says, "Me too."

I guess I got it right. She felt what I couldn't say.

I turn, dig into my duffle, pull out a small box, and flip up the lid. I drop the ring into my palm, turn back to her, and lift her left hand. As I slide on the ring – it fuckin' fits – I say, "Merry Christmas, baby. You're the gift I didn't dare to dream I'd ever have."

I had one of the admins write one my checks for a chunk of cash, and Niles brought the wad over to the house. Yesterday, that cash did a lot of talking at New York City's diamond district. Which is why Theresa is now looking down at a princess-cut diamond surrounded by two smaller diamonds set in platinum. Her mouth is open in the shape of a small O.

She looks up at me, blinks a few times, then throws herself at me, gets up on tiptoes, and pulls my head down to hers.

This time her kiss says it all.

Against her lips I say, "Love you, Theresa."

Against my lips she says, "Love you, Ethan. Be safe and hurry home."

***

With my duffle slung over my shoulder, I stuff my hands into my jacket pockets. When Theresa was in the bathroom, I strapped on my weapon in its ankle holster. In the lobby, I sat in a corner and relocated my weapon to my jacket pocket. The minute I step out of the building onto the sidewalk, I feel the hairs on the back of my neck stand up.

Shit. Someone had to've been sitting on the hotel all night. For this very reason, I'd made Theresa promise she wouldn't leave the room for an hour. Moving NY brisk, I walk around the block and head toward the garage where my car is parked. I hand the guy my ticket, drop the duffle at my feet, and wait with my back to the wall, watching the street. When the same black panel van drives by a second time, I know it's them.

I pull out my phone and call Skip, give him my location, describe the van, and tell him to get NYPD to roll up on the garage. I assure him I won't leave until they get here.

The cruiser pulls up before my car is brought down. Both cops get out and give me chin lifts. "You *federales* getting ready to shoot up our quiet 'hood?" the shorter of the two asks. His nameplate says Carlos Lopez.

"Actually, I was thinking maybe you'd like to give me a tour of your house while one of New York's finest gets my car and drives it over to your precinct."

The tall one laughs. "Just like a fed to think we're a chauffeur service." His nameplate says John O'Reilly.

The New York City grid system can be a pain in the ass. One-way streets mean you're forced to go where you don't want to go to get to where you want to go. But today, the grid system is my friend. The garage is too far up the street for the assholes in the van to see the cop car, and now they have no choice but to come past us.

"They're here," I say, my gaze locked on the van. "Back up the cruiser." O'Reilly gets in and blocks the street in less than ten seconds. The van can't go forward, and there are cars coming up the block. I can tell these assholes aren't going to come quietly. Lopez starts walking toward the van, unsnapping the leather over his weapon when I yell, "Down."

He hits the deck and I crouch behind the entranceway to the garage as the side door of the van slides open, and a guy in a watch cap takes a shot at me. Lopez is out of sight, having wedged himself under a car. The bullet ricochets off the stone wall, the shot way too close to my head for my liking. Three guys, all in watch caps, spill out of the van and start running toward Central Park, which is about fifty yards away.

As I take off after them, I see O'Reilly on the radio and know he's calling for backup. Lopez is running behind me, and as we hit Central Park West we're forced to play dodge car as the three gunmen jump over the short stone wall that rings the park. By the time we get there, they're ghosts, but we go over anyway, and the drop is not fun. As we hit the ground, we hear people screaming in the playground to our right and take off toward Eighty-first Street, which is a main thoroughfare through the park. I hear the sirens before I see the cruisers speeding toward the park. Two mounted officers come into view. They're riding off, heading east along the north side of Eighty-first Street.

Both Lopez and I are yelling at civilians to get out of the park, as we're running in the direction of the screams. A shot is fired, and we're cutting south. I see the mounted cops heading toward what looks like a castle, and people are fleeing a pavilion next to the castle. Goddammit. We're going to be sitting ducks. The gunmen are heading to higher ground. I motion to Lopez to follow me and I head to the other side of the castle. Which means climbing steep rocks, but it'll get us around back, and might give us an advantage to neutralize these assholes.

It's not easy going, and I hear more shots. I'm guessing the mounted police got there first, and the gunmen were trying to pick them off. Finally, we get to the half wall and peer over. We're on the other side of the castle and there's no sightline to the pavilion. We go over and frog walk, keeping our backs to the wall. We come to an open space and crouch-run to a short wall where there's a walkway. I can see into the pavilion, and two of the gunmen are facing away from us, their vantage point over the park. The third gunman is watching their backs and is pacing, looking in our direction.

Do these guys really see a happy ending to this?

No sooner do I have the thought than a NYPD helicopter is flying toward us, a sharpshooter hanging out the side of the chopper.

All three gunmen hunker down in the pavilion as the chopper circles overhead. Lopez looks at me and I nod. We pop up and fire on the gunmen. Neither of our weapons have the range to hit any of them, but the purpose is to flush them out so the sharpshooter in the chopper has a chance to take them down.

From above I hear, "This is the New York City police department. Put your weapons down and come out with your hands clasped behind your necks."

One of the gunmen takes a shot at the chopper, and the sharpshooter wings the asshole, who drops like a stone. The other two turn their weapons on us, but their bullets can't reach us either. Out of the corner of my eye I see a line of cops edging up toward the pavilion, and the chopper is still circling.

In a suicide move, one of the gunmen rushes out of the pavilion shooting at me and Lopez. He gets close enough for the bullets to whizz by us, then I feel a bullet shatter bone before I see the asshole go down. My right arm is dangling at an odd angle and I know I have a few minutes of shock before the pain sets in.

With weapons drawn, the line of cops surrounds the remaining asshole, who lowers his gun and lays it on the ground, then kneels and locks his fingers behind his neck.

It's not the pain that has me worried, it's the blood pooling next to my boots. Lopez is telling me to lie down, but I'm dizzy and can't seem to make my feet work. I think I hear the chopper landing, and then the ground is coming up to meet my face.

New York City
Theresa
Unexpected New Friends

About ten cop cars go speeding by as I head out of the hotel to get into a taxi the doorman hailed for me. As I slam the door close, I ask the cabbie, "You know what's going on?"

He gives me a half shrug and says, "New York. There's always something going on. Where to?"

After I give him the address of the hotel in SoHo, I lean back and hold out my left hand to admire my *engagement* ring. The ten best hours of my life play in slow motion in my brain. From his letters, I knew Ethan had to be sexy. But when I "met" him in Boston, I couldn't believe the guy I fell for has an Olympic swimmer's body, is cologne model gorgeous, and is into me in a big way.

He kisses like it's sex. Yes, I know it can be a lead-up to sex, and is definitely a part of sex, but I'm saying the kiss itself is orgasmic. And he means it to be. Some guys go with the flow, let the mood take them through the act. Some guys put on a show, and everything is positioned and practiced. But Ethan has focus. Each and every kiss, caress, touch, stroke gets his undivided attention. When he's moving inside me, he's intense in a way I've never known. It's like his whole reason for being alive is to ensure my pleasure.

And he's sweet. Loving. Tender.

After months of telling him all kinds of stories, I know he's attentive and intuitive, but I expected a man who was less in touch with his emotions. Sure, his caveman DNA quotient is high, but he lets it all hang out. If he feels it, he shows it. If something needs saying, he doesn't hesitate to lay it out. He's an excellent communicator even if sometimes he uses only one well-chosen word or sound. His grunts have different meanings, and I have about five down already.

He loves me, and he tells me in a variety of ways. Exhibit A, this engagement ring. Classy, not flashy. Elegant and timeless. How he knew what I would've chosen for myself, I have no idea, but early indications are, when it comes to me, my man pays close attention.

Him leaving today broke my heart. Our time together was too good, and neither of us wanted it to end.

"Here you go, lady."

I look out the window and we're in front of my hotel. I pay the cabbie, thank him, and get out of the taxi. Back to life with Ethan being away, and me carrying on until he comes home.

As promised, I'd called Laura after Ethan left, and didn't say much more than I'd meet her in the lobby at eleven-thirty. I'm in my room long enough to get out of yesterday's clothes and into the hotel's thick terrycloth robe when there's a knock at my door.

Before I can ask *Who's there?* my sister yells, "Open up, Ter."

She knows me well. If I tell her I'm meeting her at eleven-thirty, it means I need an hour to get ready. I look at the clock on the nightstand, and sure enough, it's ten thirty-five.

I open the door, and she barges in while ordering, "Details. Now."

No words are necessary. I wiggle the fingers of my left hand, and she lets out a screech. Then she grabs my hand and gives the ring a serious going-over.

"Ho-lee shit. He's not fooling around."

"Nope."

Now she gives me the once-over. Twice. "You look well fucked. It's about bloody time."

"Amen to that."

"When do I get to—"

My phone ringing cuts her off.

"Him?"

I shake my head, look down and see "Unknown." Maybe it is Ethan.

"Hello."

"Theresa, this is Skip."

I feel the blood rush out of my face at the same time my knees lock. My sister sees it, grabs my hand, and pushes me down to sit on the edge of the bed.

I can barely speak. "Is he alive?"

"Absolutely," he says quickly.

The breath returns to my lungs and I'm able to think. Sort of. "What happened?"

"He was shot in the arm, and he's in surgery at Mount Sinai Hospital."

"I'm leaving right now."

"They expect the surgery to take a few hours."

"I'm leaving right now."

"Gotcha. Listen, don't freak when you see cops and agents in the waiting room."

Now I'm freaking. "Okay."

"The doctor knows to ask for you."

That saves me one hurdle I don't have to clear. "Okay."

"Theresa. He's going to be all right."

"I'm holding you to that."

"I'm not BS-ing you. He'll be fine."

"Thank you for the call, Skip."

"Can't wait to meet you."

"Are you there?"

"No. I'll be there tomorrow."

"See you then."

He hangs up.

I stare at the phone and Laura takes it out of my hand. "Talk to me," she says gently.

"Ethan's an FBI agent working on a big case. He left less than two hours ago and I have no idea where he was going. His boss told me he was shot in the arm, and he's in surgery. I need to get dressed and go to Mount Sinai Hospital."

"Let me get Baz."

"Huh?"

"Get dressed and wait for me," she orders in her mom voice. "I'll be back with Baz in five minutes, and we'll all go to the hospital."

"You don't have to come. Go out and enjoy New York."

"You're off your mind right now. I get that. But you'd be all kinds of crazy if you think I'm not going to sit with my sister in a hospital waiting room while my almost brother-in-law is in surgery because he was shot."

My sister. Even while I *am* all kinds of crazy, she makes me smile.

"Right. I'll wait for you and Baz."

***

Skip said I'd see cops and agents. He didn't say I'd see a platoon of cops and agents.

When we walk into the surgical waiting room, there isn't an empty seat, and the walls are lined with stone-faced people leaning, but who appear ready to pounce at the same time.

Before I was shot, I hadn't had much contact with law enforcement, but what I knew of them didn't leave a good taste in my mouth. Three female patients had traumatic incidents with officers who'd scared the shit out of them. The cops had exerted power and authority in completely inappropriate ways. One of my patients had been pulled over on a highway at night when she was driving to her parents' house. She hadn't been speeding, but the cop made her get out of her car and sit in his cruiser. He creeped her out, and she thought if he expected a blowjob or something else, she'd turn him off if she started crying. She sat there sobbing for ten minutes before he let her go.

The cops who handled my case were decent, kind, understanding, and thorough. I'd like to believe their behavior was more than treating a victim with care. This sizeable turnout for Ethan surely represents the thin blue line standing up for their own, but if Ethan is any indication of the character of some of people in law enforcement, then much like the general population, bad cops make it hard for good cops to do their jobs.

Laura is holding my hand on one side and Baz is holding my hand on the other. Every head swings our way, and the expressions of these hardened people becomes soft. At the same time, three cops stand and motion for us to take their seats. My butt barely hit the padding when a tall woman who looks like she eats nails for breakfast comes over and squats in front of me.

"Hello, Dr. Calapiano." Her voice is much softer than I expect. "I'm Nadine Collier, the special agent in charge of the Joint Terrorism Task Force in New York."

Joint Terrorism Task Force. Ethan had told me he worked for them when we met in Boston, but only now does the weight of it sink in.

"Ah, hi." I'm tongue-tied, but I haven't forgotten my manners. "This is my sister, Laura, and her husband, Sebastian Davies."

"Sorry we have to meet under these circumstances," she says to them, and Baz nods.

The seat next to me is vacated and Nadine sits down. "Ethan went into surgery ninety minutes ago. We were told to expect the surgery to last eight hours."

My throat closes and I clasp my hands together in my lap. Something more serious than getting shot in the arm happened. My breakfast is getting ready to make a reappearance. I pull in a deep breath through my nose and ask my feet, "Do you know what happened?"

"There was a shooting incident in Central Park between the NYPD and three gunmen who had been following Ethan. He and the NYPD gave pursuit, and he was shot in the arm by one of the gunmen, all of whom have been taken into custody."

After the up-close and in-person violence I've experienced, you'd think this wouldn't shock me. But the thought of Ethan being involved in a shootout in Central Park seems unbelievable. That he got hurt is almost incomprehensible.

I nod and say, "Eight hours is a long time. Do you know why?"

"Not all of it. I know his humerus," she taps her arm between her shoulder and

elbow, "is involved, and that it takes time to remove bullets and bullet fragments before the doctors can begin repair."

Right. You'd think I'd know this, but getting me breathing as close to normal was everyone's focus. I never asked about the surgery, or bullet removal. Maybe I should have.

I raise my head and glance around the room. Everyone is watching me, but trying not to look like they're watching me. "Do you know all these people?"

She shakes her head. "No. A few of my agents who've worked with Ethan are here. I know the commanding officer from the twentieth precinct, where these officers are from."

"They're the ones who went into the park with him?"

"Yes." She gives me a small smile. "If it's all right with you, their commanding officer, Captain Washington, would like to come over to speak to you."

"Sure," I say.

She sticks her hand in her suit jacket pocket, and then hands me her business card. "My cell number is on the back. If there's anything you need, please don't hesitate to call me."

"Okay," I whisper. "Thank you. I appreciate you taking the time to talk to me."

"Any time. Ethan's one of ours."

I nod and watch her walk over to a man who makes her look like a cupcake. I've never seen as hard or square a jaw on a human being in my life.

Laura leans in and says, "She's one tough broad." Laura has super mom hearing and has always been nosy. She used to tell me all sorts of things she learned through her eavesdropping. I'm sure she heard every word of Nadine's and my conversation. "And he," she lifts her chin in the direction of Captain Washington, "seems like he could stop a bullet by looking at it." She does a fake shiver. "Scary."

My sister. I can't help but chuckle.

Captain Washington heads my way and even his gait says *Don't fuck with me.* With his hand he indicates the vacant chair. "May I?"

Dahuhuh...damn. His voice is pure sex.

Laura squeezes my knee and I turn my head and scowl at her, before looking up at him and say, "Please."

He sits and leans toward me. "I'm sorry Ethan was shot, but I'm assured he'll be fine. The worst part is the waiting. I've been in too many waiting rooms over the years, and I know this part sucks. Once he's up and talking to you, the tension, nausea, and apprehension will go away. He'll recover, and while he's doing it, he'll be a pain in your ass."

I smile at him and say, "Something to look forward to."

He smiles back, and it's amazing. All the hard goes out of his face and I'm staring at white teeth and eyes full of mischief. With that voice and smile, he must get a lot of action.

As if he read my mind he says, "Years ago, I fell down the basement stairs a few days after my wife and I moved into our home. Broke my collarbone. She yelled at me the minute the doctor let her into my room. That's how I knew I was going to be all right."

"I'll keep that in mind."

He tilts his head and says, "They're not going to leave. He stood by one of ours and kept him safe."

"Sounds like Ethan."

"Yeah." He stands. "The officer, Carlos Lopez, wants a word. That okay with you?"

"Of course."

"I've gotta go, but I'll be back tomorrow to give your man shit."

He's a charmer. "I think you and Ethan are going to be friends."

"Count on it." He turns and walks out of the waiting room.

I look around and see a female officer sitting across and down from me who seems to be guarding me. "Bathroom," I mouth.

She gets up and waves me to follow. Of course, Laura joins us.

***

Captain Washington is right. The waiting sucks. Carlos Lopez hung out with us for a while talking about nothing in particular, but clearly feeling the need to keep close. Over time, a few officers left, but most stayed.

Different officers got food and distributed sandwiches or bags of chips, sodas, coffee, and bottles of water. Their comings and goings were the rhythm of the day.

At eight at night, some nine and a half hours after Ethan went into surgery, two doctors come out and one calls out, "Dr. Calapiano?"

After keeping vigil for so long, I didn't want to exclude the officers who had done their best to keep me, Laura, and Baz fed – I hardly ate – and hydrated.

I stood and walked to the doctors, but stopped at the edge of the waiting room, indicating that they could talk to me in front of everyone. Laura and Baz stood on either side of me.

"Right," the female doctor says. "I'm Dr. Margolis. I'm a vascular surgeon. The bullet hit a brachial vein before shattering the humerus. I repaired the vein, and Dr. Pritari, an orthopedic surgeon, repaired the bone."

That seems to be all she's willing to share.

Dr. Pritari says, "We had to clean out the area to prevent lead toxicity, and the vein had to be clamped while we repaired the bone. We used as many of the bone fragments as we could, and repositioned them with the bone into its normal alignment. As is frequently the case with this type of injury, the length of the bone was reduced. With Ethan we were able to keep the reduction to under four millimeters. The bone is being held together with two plates, and screws, which will remain inside his body. After I finished with the implants, Dr. Margolis was able to repair the vein. She's quite skilled."

I like him better than her, but if she put Ethan's vein back together, I don't care if she has the bedside manner of a rock.

"Ethan will remain in the hospital for about three days," Dr. Pritari continues. "I've written down the names of a few of our colleagues in the Boston area. Once you choose, Ethan will have his follow-up appointments with them, and when appropriate, the orthopedist will send Ethan to physical therapy. Do you have any questions?"

Yeah. Why didn't I keep him in the hotel room with me for another ten days?

"Did the blood loss affect his organs?" I knew this was something the doctors monitored religiously with me, especially given where I was shot.

"Fortunately, the officers at the scene acted quickly and tied off a tourniquet, and Ethan was brought here by helicopter. We don't anticipate any lasting effects."

I looked back at Carlos and knew he'd saved Ethan's arm. I wonder which one of these cops flew Ethan to the hospital.

Baz asks, "How long before he regains full use of his arm?"

Dr. Pritari bobs his head a little. "Some people don't, but Ethan's fit and strong, so I have high hopes. The bone should knit within eight weeks. The real work will be in PT. If he does what he's told and keeps all his appointments, he'll heal in the four-to-six month range."

I move forward and place my hand on Dr. Pritari's arm. "Thank you." Then I turn to Dr. Margolis and hold out my hand. She gives it a brisk shake, and I tell her, "Thank you."

Dr. Pritari reaches in the deep pocket of his lab coat and pulls out a business card. "Call me if you have any more questions."

I take the card and stuff it into my jeans pocket. "When can I see him?"

Dr. Pritari says, "He should be out of recovery soon. Go to the waiting room on the eighth floor. Someone will come out to get you when he's been moved into his room."

He and Dr. Margolis leave and I turn, walk to Carlos, and give him a big hug. "Thank you. I know it was you who saved his arm."

"Returning the favor. He kept me safe."

I have a feeling there's more to that statement, but I don't want to know. I turn to the room. "Thank you for staying here with us. I can't tell you how much it means having your support." I draw in a deep breath. "Is the helicopter pilot here?"

"No, hon," a tall thin cop answers. "He had to stay on duty. But we'll let him know you said thank you."

I nod and tell them, "Please, go home. Eat some real food and get some sleep."

Over the next few minutes cops come up to me and say good night until it's Baz, Laura, me, and Carlos left.

"You should go home," I tell Carlos. "You had a rough day."

"I will after he wakes up and I stick my head in to say a few words."

"Deal."

We walk down the hall, get into an elevator, and Baz hits the button for the eighth floor.

***

"We can't," I tell Ethan while sitting astride his lap in the hospital bed. I grab his beard at his chin and yank. He scowls and pulls his head back. "Now that I have your attention—"

"Babe. You're sitting on my dick. My arm is wrapped around you. I can see you. I've tasted that sweet mouth, and I can smell your hair. How do you not have my attention?"

"You're ignoring the point."

"Which is?"

"If we stay at your place, it's a shorter ride to the doctors and the better hospitals if we need them."

He sighs. "How many rooms in your townhouse?"

"Six."

"How many bathrooms?"

"One and a half."

"I have a one-bed, one-bath apartment with a living room-kitchen combo. No back patio. No upstairs terrace. No parks down the street, no garage, and no closet space. We are not living there for the once every three months I have to see a doctor, and I'm sure as fuck not going to need to be in a hospital after they let me out of here tomorrow. They fixed what was broken and I'm moving on."

"I see you took my advice."

I know that velvet silky voice. I turn my head and Omar Washington is standing in the doorway to Ethan's room.

"I did," I grin.

"Hey, man." Omar walks to the bed and slaps Ethan on the leg. "She bitching at you?'

Ethan shakes his head. "You tell her to do that shit?"

"You worried she's going to bust out crying every time she looks at that sling?"

"Point taken."

I lean in and touch my lips to Ethan's. "I don't need to be here for the caveman conversation. I'm going to make some calls." I climb off Ethan, grab my bag, and then walk around the bed and touch my cheek to Omar's. "Thank you," I whisper.

"Any time, every time, Ter."

I walk out of the room, wave to the nurses as I pass their hub, and go to the family room at the end of the hall and close the door. The difference between forty-two hours ago and now is night and day. After he was brought up from recovery, Ethan woke up in his hospital room long enough to say thank you to Carlos, hello to Baz and Laura, and to order me into bed beside him. Then he passed out and didn't wake up again until nine the next morning, even though the nurses came in every couple of hours to take his blood pressure, check his drain, take his temperature, and look for blood in his Foley bag.

After his doctors had come by and did their checks, the head surgical resident came in and did her check, and everyone said the catheter could be removed, the nurses came in and did just that, to which Ethan let up an unhappy groan, and then a sigh of relief.

Carlos came back. Omar came back. Laura and Baz hung out for a couple of hours – they love Ethan – and then they had to head home.

Skip came by mid-afternoon and stayed for a few hours. After our initial hello, how do you do conversation, I left them alone behind a closed door for over two hours. Skip left before dinner, and by yesterday evening, Ethan was himself again, except on pain meds.

This morning the nurses disconnected his IV, his doctors came by and said they planned to release him tomorrow, a physical therapist did a consult and showed Ethan in what position the sling was optimum, then the PT went with Ethan as he took his first long walk.

Now Omar is here – I knew he and Ethan would become fast friends – and for the first time since showing off my ring to Laura in SoHo, my heart isn't in my throat, my stomach isn't in knots, and my lungs don't feel constricted.

Ethan's moving in with me and giving up his apartment, which is month to month, and he's already given his thirty-day notice. He's on leave from work until his doctors clear him for light duty, sometime after two months from now when the orthopedist is sure the bone has knitted.

I promised myself I wouldn't make him crazy. I'm going back to work on Thursday, but I'm seeing only six patients a day until I'm sure *I'm* okay with being away from him. I tuck myself into the corner of the sofa and go through my email, then I check in with my receptionist, who's been a magician at rearranging my calendar, then I call Laura.

"How is he?" This is how she answers the phone.

"Omar's visiting so I left them to each other 'cause the testosterone in the room was choking me."

"They cutting him loose tomorrow?"

"We should be on our way home by eleven. I figure I should be to you between one-thirty and two o'clock."

"Perfect. I'll give the girls lunch regular time, have Mom pick them up at one. This way it'll be quiet when you guys get here and we can eat in peace before Mom comes back at three and bedlam ensues."

My sister. Always looking out for me, and now Ethan.

"Thanks, Laurie."

"Love you, Ter."

She hangs up, and I go to my new favorite website: Marguerite Sells Mendon. Every day, I scroll through the listings, and so far she hasn't added any new houses, but I know our home is out there.

Holy shit. She's added a new house. Set back from the road. Not in the woods, but there are lots of trees. It's stone, and it's older, not from colonial times, but with that look. It has a wide front porch with thick white columns. I zip through the photos of the interior and go to the ones of the back of the house. There it is. A traditional conservatory with multipaned windows and an angled glass ceiling. I jump up, run out of the room, turn around, go back, grab my bag, run out again, and nearly skip down the hall to Ethan's room.

I stand in the doorway wagging my phone back and forth, and Ethan stops telling Omar the Yankees are going to suck next season.

"Babe?"

"I found it."

"Found what?"

"Our home." I dash over to the bed and shove the phone in his face. He takes it from me and starts scrolling with his thumb.

"It's a money pit."

"It has a conservatory."

"Babe. Have you looked at the inside of the house?"

"Not yet. It has a conservatory."

"Theresa. The kitchen and bathrooms need to be updated. The floors need to be stripped, sanded, and re-varnished, and the driveway needs to be repaved. And that's what I can see from looking at these tiny-ass pictures."

Omar looks like he's about to bust out laughing.

"Shut it," I tell Omar. "Don't encourage him." I grab my phone. "I'll call her. We'll go see it this weekend."

He shakes his head. "Okay, baby."

I know he figures once I see how much needs to be done to the place, I'll relent. Little does he know. It's on an acre and a half of land. It has mature trees, and it has a fabulous conservatory.

"Great."

I leave the room and call Marguerite.

Dutchford
Ethan
No Loose Threads

There'll be a lot of things that cross the doorstep of the twenty-four-hundred-square-foot never-ending home improvement project we bought, but fear and evil won't be included on that list.

Skip had brought unbelievable news that day he came to see me in the hospital. The guy who'd gotten winged by the chopper sniper turned out to be a songbird. As luck would have it, the asshole is a U.S citizen, born in Brighton Beach to Russian parents. The family is all tied up with the Lebedevsky *Bratva*. The guy was in the Jacob Javits Federal building to apply for a new passport, but he had the wrong building. He saw me in the lobby and called his *Vory* in Brighton Beach to tell them Alexei Berenikoff was in New York. It seems Alexei and I could be brothers, if not twins.

Apparently, my distant relatives in Russia who live in and around St. Petersburg are not the kind of family I'd want to claim. Not *Bratva*, but small-time crooks, thieves, and murders nonetheless. Alexei, a contract killer, was allegedly in New York to knock off one of the Lebedevsky *Vory*. Skip and I opined whoever sent him wanted someone unknown on the job. It seems he's more known than his contractor thought.

As I'd surmised, the three gunmen had been sitting on my hotel because the songbird was ordered to follow me. They thought they were taking out Alexei.

They had the wrong Berenikoff.

Since the one gunman who hadn't been shot saw me collapse in a pool of blood, he told anyone who would carry the message back to the *Vory* that Alexei was dead. Somehow, the three morons thought the NYPD was trying to arrest Alexei and that he was running after the gunmen to kill them before the NYPD got him.

Included in the tune the songbird had sung was the name of the *Vory* in New York who's the mastermind for the dope-and-rope operation going on predominantly in New England. While the JTTFs don't have intel on the extent of the network, they now know it exists and are taking measures to bring it down at the same time they intend to chop off the head of the snake.

I'm out of that now. When I returned to work in light duty status, I was desk bound and assigned to Intelligence. The work is interesting and is a bit Sherlock Holmes-esque in that we piece clues together to understand the picture. Mostly though, knowing what's at stake if I went back to the JTTF, my life with my Flower takes precedence over getting the adrenaline rush from field work.

I'm getting all the rush I need at home.

One of my favorite nights so far was not long after I'd been released from the hospital, and Theresa had come home to find me clean shaven. I didn't have to lose the mustache and beard, but I don't want to be mistaken for Alexei, or any other Russian-born Berenikoff, ever again.

She knew my routine and met me and Boo in the park, where we were playing Frisbee. I'll never forget her reaction. She put her hands on my cheeks and said, "Holy shit. You're beautiful. I mean, I loved the beard, and thought you were hot before, but look at you. You're stunning."

"Tell me more."

"Let's go home and I'll show you instead."

Remember incentivizing through reward? That's how Theresa got me to agree to buy the money pit. She never asked me to do it. She never brought up the house again after we'd spent an hour walking through and around it. But after a week of the most incredible blowjobs – my Flower knows how to use her talented mouth on my cock – I would've surfed naked on the Charles River in January for her.

We're packing up the townhouse. Six months after the shooting, I'm doing well in PT, and I don't have to wear the sling anymore, but my arm is at about seventy percent. I can pack, but I can't lift more than the coffeepot with my right hand. Not yet.

"Ethan," Theresa shouts from upstairs.

"Yeah, babe."

"I'm sending Boo down to you. He's messing with the clothes in the suitcases as I'm packing."

The dog plays her. He knows she's sweeter than sugar and he takes advantage. He doesn't do that shit with me. I whistle and he comes running down the steps. I give him a treat and tell him to go lie down on his bed in the living room. Off he goes, happy to oblige.

I go back to checking the boxes' contents, sealing them, numbering them and entering the contents next to the box's number in my moving log. It's going to be crazy enough in that house without ripping open every box to try to find where we put shit.

As I'm bent over a box, I hear Theresa's footfall on the stairs. A minute later she's behind me caressing my ass.

"You want some of that, baby?"

"I always want some of this," she purrs.

Damn. The sound of her throaty, sexy voice gets me hard.

She unbuckles my belt, unzips my jeans, and pulls them down to my thighs. Then she turns around, pulls down her yoga pants, and wiggles her fantastic ass at me. I bend her at the waist with my left arm and start working her pussy with the fingers of my right hand. This, I have no trouble doing. She's squirming and moaning as I get her wet, and just as I position my dick at her entrance, the doorbell rings.

"Ignore it," she rasps out.

My baby wants some of me and she's going to get it. I sink in and she grips the lip of the counter. We're ungloved. After all the blood tests I had in the hospital, we know I'm clean, and Theresa took a test more for her peace of mind than mine.

Damn, she's hot and wet, and she works me up so fast, I can feel my balls tighten up.

The doorbell rings again.

I keep driving into *my* sweet pussy, and I'm close. I reach around and squeeze her clit, then brush it lightly. She's panting my name. I squeeze again and she pushes back, letting out a low moan as her spasming pulls it out of me.

I collapse on her back and huff, "You're a great lay, baby."

She laughs and I hold her tight to keep her from pushing me out of her body.

The doorbell rings again, accompanied by knocking, which gets Boo up and barking.

"Do you think if we stay quiet whoever it is will think only the dog is home?"

"It's worth a try," I say into her ear.

The doorbell rings again, more knocking, and a muffled shout that sounds like, "Ter, you home?"

Shit. Slowly I pull out and I stuff myself into my pants. "I'll get it."

I hear Theresa move to the downstairs bathroom, and I buckle my belt before I look at the iPad next to the door. Yeah, I upped the security on the townhouse, and our new place will have even more.

The woman on the screen is definitely a Calapiano. She's a lot taller than Theresa, and has short hair, but she shares many of Theresa's and Laura's characteristics. I tell Boo to go lie down and he circles once before he heads back into the living room.

I open the door and the woman asks with wide eyes, "Who are you?"

"Ethan. Theresa's man."

Her head jerks back. "No shit."

"No shit."

I lean forward to pick up the large suitcase sitting on the stoop next to her, and she tells me in an accusatory tone, "You smell like sex."

I look at my boots and grin. *Sure do.*

As I'm placing the suitcase in the hallway, Theresa comes to the door and yells, "Oh my god. Max. What are you doing here?"

So this is Max.

"I've run away from home," Max mutters.

Theresa leans against my side and says, "Holy shit."

ABOUT THE AUTHOR

Elle Wright has been writing stories since she was a child, which led her to a career in journalism. She enjoys reporting life as much as making up a world she can control. She lives on the east coast of the United States where most of her large, noisy family resides. When she isn't in front of her computer, she loves to travel, garden, hang out with her dogs, and take in the brisk sea air that she's told is supposed to help calm her. She's been testing that theory for a while now.

CONNECT WITH ELLE:
Twitter: @ElleWright18
Instagram: @Elle_Wright_Writes
FB: facebook.com/elle.wright.1460

www.BOROUGHSPUBLISHINGGROUP.com

If you enjoyed this book, please write a review. Our authors appreciate the feedback, and it helps future readers find books they love. We welcome your comments and invite you to send them to info@boroughspublishinggroup.com. Follow us on Facebook, Twitter and Instagram, and be sure to sign up for our newsletter for surprises and new releases from your favorite authors.

Are you an aspiring writer? Check out www.boroughspublishinggroup.com/submit and see if we can help you make your dreams come true.